# AGE OF THE SON

## LEE BEZOTTE

INSPARKET
MEDIA

*This book is for all who believe that faith is spelled R-I-S-K.*

# CHAPTER ONE
## A DARK DREAM

"I'm scared!" Son cried out.

His voice echoed into the darkness, and a feeling of helplessness wrapped itself around his shoulders.

For several nights, the boy had the same dream. The world was black all around him, and in the blackness hid men of conscienceless evil who were waiting for an opportune time to pounce upon him.

As he stood there, a wind began to pick up and the sound of rustling could be heard. The rustling grew to a strange clamor, and it raised Son's fear until he was unable to move his feet or unsheathe his sword.

"Help!" the boy shouted. "Someone, please!"

From the darkness, a wheezing laughter arose. It sent chills down his back.

The laughter turned to mocking as voices rang out: "Help me! I'm scared! Ha-ha-hah!"

"Leave me alone!" Son returned, trying to sound courageous. But the cackling continued.

Finally, he was able to pull his sword from its scabbard. He held it out and demanded, "Show yourself!"

At that, the wind only blew more furiously and the mocking voices became even louder.

Amidst the commotion, the boy noticed a strange sound. It was almost imperceptible, and he thought perhaps it was the wind blowing in a peculiar way, or the wicked harmonies of the men's voices playing tricks with his ears.

It was the sound of a whisper. He couldn't tell what it was saying at first, so he strained to block out all the other voices and hone in on the quiet words that were being spoken.

"It's okay," the soft voice spoke. It then repeated slowly, "It is okay."

Son couldn't tell which direction the voice came from. He only knew that the more he drew his attention to it, the clearer it became, and the boisterous taunting held an ever-weakening grasp upon him.

The simple words repeated, and each time Son heard them, they seemed to wash over him with ever-increasing peace until he finally recognized the voice.

"Great Father!" he called out.

Suddenly, he was pulled from his sleep when a loud knock rang through the door of his cottage.

## CHAPTER TWO
# A FAREWELL OF SORTS

Son pulled his shirt over his head as he ran down the stairs. Galloping through the kitchen toward the door, he noticed Maren sitting at the table eating a piece of toast. "Why didn't you answer the door?" he asked the girl.

"I don't know," she shrugged, and took another bite of her toast.

"Who's there?" the boy yelled through the door.

"A wind from the north," Dulnear called back.

Son smiled and threw open the door. As he did a large, cat-like beast leapt upon him. It was so large that only the front part of its body could get through the entrance, and it knocked him to the floor. "No!" he shouted, and tried to wrestle himself out from under the furry animal. Before he knew it, he was being licked across the face by an odorous tongue that felt like a sharpening stone.

"Aww, she likes you," the man from the north assured from the outside.

"Well, she tried to eat me," the boy retorted.

"But then she saved you," Dulnear replied. He patted the animal on its backside and said something in northern-speak. When he did, it backed out of the doorway and sat in the grass. The man from the north ducked through the door, crouched next to Son, and extended his hand to help him to his feet. "Just do not tell Faymia about the part where it bit into your shoulder," he whispered.

Faymia followed Dulnear into the house. "Why did you let her pounce on him like that?" she snipped. "She's going to stink up the whole kitchen."

The cat-monster flopped its enormous body to the ground outside. It then released a breathy yawn, exposing its long, sharp fangs. Son felt uneasy about having it nearby. His wounds had barely recovered from his encounter with the beast in the Petraig Mountains.

"Kitty!" Maren whispered excitedly. She tiptoed around her friends and went out to the beast to scratch its chin.

"This is my friend Verrox," Dulnear announced to the girl. "She is a kottur from Tuas-arum."

Maren stroked the kottur's shaggy bib. Next to the enormous beast, she looked like a wee toddler. She suppressed a smile of excitement and said in a low, raspy voice, "Verrox the kottur, queen of the northern mountains."

"All right," Faymia said in a clear voice. "Our apologies for the excitement. We were wondering if we could speak with the two of you."

"Sure," Son answered. "I was just about to make some breakfast. Would you like some?"

"Absolutely!" Dulnear smiled.

Son grabbed a basket and ran out the door to collect

some eggs from the hen house. As he did, he hoped that the kottur hadn't already eaten the hens.

As the four of them sat around the table, Son managed to forget about the strange dream he had the night before. "I can't believe that beast followed you here. You must smell like its mother!" he teased Dulnear as he scooped another spoonful of scrambled egg into his mouth.

"Very funny, boy!" the northerner barked. "How do you know she was not following YOU?"

"Because I didn't feed her at the Petraig Mountains," the boy retorted.

"You did WHAT?" Faymia chimed in.

Dulnear began to stumble over his words. "Well... you see..."

Faymia shook her head and laughed, "Warrior from the north, soft on furry animals!"

"Soft on furry animals!" Maren repeated with a giggle. She was sitting in the farthest seat at the table so she could see out the door and watch the kottur. It was now dozing in the grass, flipping its tail occasionally as it snored into the late-morning air.

"You really like Verrox, don't you?" Faymia asked the girl.

"Uh-huh," she nodded. "I want to ride her." She then smiled brightly with her eyes as she pressed her hands together.

"Well, do not be too hasty," Dulnear advised. "She is a

wild animal, after all. She does not belong to us. She is her own."

"Okay," Maren murmured, and continued to gaze out at the animal.

As Son observed the interactions between his unlikely family, his heart beamed and all felt right with the world. It had been a long time since they had simply been together, and he wished he could slow down time and make the moment last all day.

"That is an interesting smile," Dulnear observed as he put his arm around the boy. "What is on your mind?"

"Oh, I'm just grateful, I reckon," Son answered.

"As am I," the man from the north replied. "As am I." He then breathed in deeply and released a long, satisfied exhale.

"Actually," Faymia interrupted. "We really need to talk with the two of you about a matter of importance."

Dulnear sat up straight, looked into Son's eyes, then glanced back at his wife. "Do we have to right now?" he asked.

"I'm afraid we do," she lamented.

Son immediately knew what his friends wanted to talk about, and dreaded it. He knew they needed to discuss the slaver king, but he wanted to pretend the evil man didn't exist. With everything in his being, he wanted to live as he was in this present moment; happy, safe, and loved.

"So you see," Dulnear continued. "They are coming.

Brunnlyn and the Saor have been keeping a watchful eye out. The storm is inevitable."

The man from the north had explained how Ocmallum, the slave king, was likely to descend upon Gale Hill Farm in the coming days, and that the wretch was obsessed with making an example out of Son and Maren.

The boy sighed. He felt as if all the energy had been drained from his body. Rubbing his temple with his right hand he asked, "What should we do?"

"That is a very good question," the warrior responded. "Faymia and I believe that running would be a slow death. But staying to fight could mean the end as well. We are against all odds. What do you believe to be the best course of action?"

Dulnear then peered into Son's eyes. It was a look the boy had not seen before, and it was accompanied by a strange feeling. The world around him seemed to shift. The air became thick and difficult to breathe, and the floor beneath his feet seemed to sway like a boat on shallow water.

"I know what I must do, but I'm afraid to do it," Son confessed.

Dulnear sighed deeply through his nostrils. He held his gaze and waited.

"I agree that fleeing would be no kind of living," the boy continued. "And staying to fight would most likely be the end of us all." He then turned and focused his eyes on the dreary sky beyond the kitchen window. "But in fighting, there is the possibility that we could end slavery in Aun."

Faymia reached across the table and placed her hand on

Son's arm. There was a tear in her eye as she spoke in a low voice. "That's a tremendous risk, and a lofty ambition. But it's one that I would stand with you in."

The man from the north leaned in closer to the boy's face. His visage seemed to fill the entirety of his vision. "So..." he began.

"We fight!" Maren broke in.

Son jerked his eyes toward his young friend. He was surprised to see that she was so willing to do battle with slavers.

"Why are we even talking about it?" the young girl continued. Her cheeks burned red and her eyes grew deadly serious. "If we do nothing, then how many more will be tricked into slavery like Faymia and me? If *we* don't fight them, then who will?"

Dulnear shook his head. A grim smile crept over his lips. "I suppose it is not every day that the slaver king and the whole of his company come knocking at your door. If ever there was an opportunity to end his evil trade, this is it."

Son was filled with fear, but he knew this was somehow a sacred moment. He was aware that their actions had the potential to change the land forever. With trembling in his voice, he muttered, "I want to stay and fight."

"All right then," Dulnear nodded. His face looked like it was set in stone, and he drew a deep breath. "We shall stand together here and do battle."

Son swallowed. Now that he had made his decision, he felt even more uncertain. "What do we do first?" he asked his friend.

"We go to Laor and warn the town," he answered. "They must know what trouble is coming."

## CHAPTER THREE
# A GRIM WARNING

S on and Dulnear stood at the entrance to the pub at Laor. Though nothing had changed since his last visit, the boy felt the atmosphere around him to be strangely different. It was like a portrait of a man whose eyes were slightly off, causing the observer to feel a sense of unease.

"Greetings, Henry," the man from the north announced as they approached the bar.

"Hello there, northerner," the man behind the counter returned. "And Son," he added.

The room was quiet with the usual early afternoon lull. A few patrons visited with each other over their brew, and there was a man at the table in the corner that seemed to be lost in the task of writing in an empty journal.

"Are you here to sell more of your creations?" Henry asked the boy as he toweled out a wet stein.

"No," Son answered. He wanted to state their business at the pub but wasn't sure how to begin.

"Stout, please," Dulnear ordered, interrupting the boy's thoughts.

"And a mead, please," Son added.

As he stood close to the bar, Son recalled his first time visiting the establishment. He remembered how the locals gawked at his enormous friend. He also remembered how he was barely tall enough to rest his chin on the bar. Now, older, taller, and stronger, he stood almost eye to eye with the barkeep, and the intimidation he once felt when interacting with adults had faded away.

As their mugs were placed on the bar in front of them, the boy watched his friend sip from his dark stout, then lick a thick layer of foam from his mustache. "What do we do?" he asked.

Dulnear turned to him and scratched at the thick hair on his chin. Glancing around the room behind Son, he grimaced and answered, "I have an idea."

"What is it?" Son asked.

"Well, a partial idea," the man from the north admitted. "We need to spread the word, but I would not want to put the village in a panic. Fear and worry make people do strange things."

Son sipped from his mug of mead and placed it back on the bar. Every action he took, after he had made the decision to stay and fight, seemed to feel as if it were being made in a dream. He tilted his head sideways and asked, "So, what's your partial idea?"

Pushing his mouth to the side, Dulnear replied in a half-whisper, "We start by talking to Henry. All paths lead to the pub, so maybe he would be able to help."

Hearing the warrior's idea, Son felt a bit better. It

seemed a far cry wiser than making an announcement in the town square.

Clearing his throat, the man from the north began, "Excuse me, Henry."

"What can I do for you?" the barkeep answered as he dried his hands on a towel that draped over his shoulder.

"Have you seen any strangers about lately?" Dulnear asked.

"No more than usual," Henry answered. "Being that we're near the only road running from the east coast to the west coast of Aun, we see a handful of strangers every day."

"Well," Dulnear went on, "do you remember when the slavers came through here a while back?"

"How can I forget?" Henry grumbled. His forehead wrinkled and his dark eyebrows pressed low against his eyes.

Trying to keep his voice to a hush, Dulnear continued, "We have it on good authority that they are headed this way again."

"What? Haven't they done enough damage?" Henry barked.

Son gestured to the barkeep to keep his voice down, but it was to no avail.

"We just need a little help calmly getting the word out," the man from the north explained as he leaned in closely to the man across the bar.

"I'll do more than get the word out!" Henry bellowed. "I'll clobber the next fella that even smells like one of those lowlifes!"

Just then, Son could hear a chair hit the wood floor and noticed two men rushing to the exit. They had hardly reached the doorway when Dulnear flung his stein, striking one of them in the back of the head, causing him to stumble into his companion. He then withdrew his sword from underneath his long fur coat and ran out of the tavern after them.

---

With sword in hand, Son ran out the door as quickly as he could. Just outside of the tavern, Dulnear was standing ready to fight the two men. They each held a small sword and continually glanced at each other as if they were hoping the other would attack first.

"Slaver scouts!" Dulnear yelled back to the boy.

Son was surprised by the appearance of the two men. The slavers he had encountered in the past were usually well-dressed, groomed, and perfumed. These men looked like any other that might pass through Laor. "How do you know?" he asked.

"The local farmers do not carry swords," he said as he kept his gaze on the strangers. "And these men look as if they have been living in the brush. They are either scouts or bounty hunters. Either way, they are not here as friends."

Son stepped a little closer. He now noticed the shabbiness of the men. Though they did not bear the usual markings of slavers, the worn-leather look on their faces and the reek of cigarette smoke was all too familiar to the boy. He gripped the hilt of his sword firmly and his jaw tightened like a vise.

"So, you are looking for us, eh?" Dulnear snarled.

The man nearest Son gave a strange smile and glared at the boy. "We are looking for *him*," he hissed.

Son's stomach turned and he willed the strength to remain on his feet as he glared back at the man.

"Well, it looks like you have found him," Dulnear declared in a clear, deep voice. "What do you plan to do with him?"

The man's lip curled as he released a growl and lunged at Son. Dulnear extended his sword to block the man's attack, but the man's companion kicked the northerner's hand, making the block ineffectual.

Fortunately, Son was able to roll out of the way, placing the man to his left. He thrust his sword toward the slaver's shoulder, but the man pivoted and brought the broad side of his blade against the side of the boy's head.

"You're worth a lot of money alive," the bounty hunter stated. "But still a handsome amount dead. Either way, you're going to make us rich."

Son rubbed the side of his face and stared at the man. As he did, he wished he had a witty retort the way Dulnear always seemed to have in situations like these. Then, it occurred to him that the man was right-handed. He also led with his right foot. The combination of those two things hinted to him that he was a novice fighter. He lunged his blade forward toward the man's abdomen. The scout instinctively blocked with a downward motion of his sword, allowing the boy to continue his motion forward with a sharp blow to his shin.

"Youch!" the man howled. He then furiously slashed upward.

Son rolled to his left and forward, avoiding the man's sword, then struck with an outward slice at the back of his leg. The man cried out in pain again and nearly fell to the ground. Before he could retaliate, the boy swung down hard on the man's hand, cutting deep and causing him to drop his sword.

Son noticed the man reach into his tunic with his left hand. He spun to his right, and with both hands on his sword, slashed left, leaving a long gash along the scout's forearm and hand.

The man now held both hands against his chest, cursing and trembling with pain. "You're going to die, kid," he wheezed.

The boy kept both hands on the handle of his sword. He wound hard to his right, then brought the flat side of blade against the man's temple, returning his attack from earlier. The man stumbled to his knees, then teetered there.

Son sheathed his sword, grabbed the back of the man's head, and drove his knee into his cheek. The man fell back unconscious, collapsing onto himself like a broken cattail.

As the boy's attention returned to his surroundings, he heard Dulnear say to him, "Not bad, lad."

Son looked over at his companion so see him casually leaning against his sword. His opponent was lying on the ground a few feet from his own severed leg. Unnerved by Dulnear's nonchalance, he asked, "How long have you been standing there?"

"Ever since the miscreant said that you were worth a lot of money alive," he answered.

"That was a while ago," the boy observed. "Why didn't you come and help me?"

"Because you were doing fine on your own," Dulnear responded. He raised an eyebrow and tilted his head. "Did I spend many months training you so that I could fight your battles?"

"I guess not," Son conceded.

The man from the north chuckled silently and stood straight. "You have learned so much, and you handled that scout expertly." He then walked over to his opponent, who was writhing on the ground as he bled freely from the place where his leg was severed from his body. "You can consider him practice for what is to come."

To the boy's shock, Dulnear quickly plunged his sword through the chest of the man and withdrew it. He then walked over to Son's adversary and did the same.

---

"What are you doing?" Son cried out.

Dulnear wiped his blade on the grass and placed it in its sheath. "What do you mean?" he asked.

"These men were properly defeated," the boy exclaimed. "You didn't need to kill them!"

The man from the north stood still and took a deep breath. He pressed his lips together and his face softened. "I know it seems that way," he began to explain. "But they would have come back. Somehow, they would have found us, or told their employer about us. And your man would have killed you had you not rendered him unconscious."

Son was torn. He had once wanted to be a great warrior, but now the whole business was distasteful to him. He wanted to keep arguing, but he knew Dulnear's words were true, no matter how disgraceful they sounded to him.

He just couldn't understand how his friend could be so casual about it all.

For a moment, he stared at the man, not knowing what to say. Then he noticed Henry the barkeep standing just outside the tavern door. He was followed out by the few patrons who were inside. They stood in silence, watching the boy and his mentor argue. "Sorry, Henry," the boy said sheepishly.

"No worries," the man replied. The bravado he displayed inside was now gone, and he winced as he observed the dead bodies on the ground.

Dulnear turned toward the small crowd and addressed them. "I suppose the time for subtlety is over," he lamented. "These men were working for the slaver king Ocmallum. They will not be the last to scout Laor, and hell will not be far behind."

"What do you mean?" one of the bar patrons asked. He was an older man who appeared as if he had gotten an early start drinking that day.

"We all remember what the slavers did to our village not long ago," the man from the north began. "They seduced and hauled off beloved family members. They took away husbands, wives, sons, and daughters. Despite our raid on the slaver camp, it was too late for some of them, and they never returned."

"I remember. I haven't seen my son ever since!" a woman called out.

"They are a plague upon Aun," Dulnear sympathized. "And now they are returning."

"Well, we won't fall for their schemes this time!" another patron yelled.

The northerner took a deep breath and glanced at Son. Addressing the crowd, which had now grown from the addition of other townsfolk across the square, he warned, "The greed of these men is unmeasurable. If they cannot gain by luring you, they will gain by force. And they will be back this time with fury." He then stepped closer to the crowd and grabbed the hilt of his sword with his left hand. Continuing, he urged, "Some of you received a second chance when you were freed from the slavers. That freedom did not come easy. It was hard-fought and bloody. Freedom comes at a price, and is kept with a price. I suggest you arm yourselves, and become proficient in combat. The days ahead will not be easy."

Several in the crowd shuffled their feet and looked at the ground. Only one man, Henry the barkeep, seemed particularly inspired. "I have a sword at home. I will not be going out without it again," he declared.

Son was moved by Dulnear's words. He had not given much thought to the ongoing effort that safekeeping one's freedom required, and many of the battles he had fought alongside his friends began to take on new meaning. Stepping closer to his friend so that his voice would not travel to the crowd, he said quietly, "These souls don't stand a chance. They're not fighters."

The man from the north turned his eyes toward the crowd, then back to the boy. "Then we will have to train them."

Son couldn't imagine being able to train the village in time for the coming conflict, but he tried to keep his hopes up the best he could. "I'll take your word for it," he murmured to his friend.

"Now, go home and tell your families to prepare. Find whatever you can use for weapons," Dulnear instructed.

"What? We're not soldiers. We're farmers!" one of the tavern patrons protested.

"You can become what you need to be when you need to be it," the man from the north countered. "Success or failure begins here and now, not in the moment of battle." He then gestured toward the barkeep and announced, "I will train Henry to fight as we northerners do, and he will return to the village and train you. If you choose not to be a part of this, then I suggest you pack your belongings and leave Laor as soon as possible. Now go!"

As the crowd dispersed, Dulnear approached Henry. "I hope I did not speak out of turn," he said. "You seem to possess a fighting spirit."

"Of course," Henry swallowed. He then squeaked out, "I'm ready to fight for Laor."

"All right, then," the warrior said. "Son and I will return to Gale Hill posthaste. You will dispose of these bodies. Leave no trace that these men were ever here. When you have completed your task, fetch the sword from your home and ride to Gale Hill Farm. Be sure that no one follows you."

"Yes, sir," the man stuttered. "Dispose of bodies."

Son and Dulnear mounted their horses and began to ride toward the road. The boy was lost in thought as the situation now sat on his shoulders with a much greater weight. The words, "What are we going to do?" seemed to escape his mouth with no conscious effort.

"We are going to need more than the locals in this fight," the northerner answered.

"What do you mean?" Son asked.

"I mean that we are going to have to recruit others if we are going to succeed," Dulnear explained.

A thought now came to the boy that brought a small amount of relief. "Do you mean like Aesef and Phel?" The boy was fond of the farmer, and remembered that he was a skilled fighter.

"Yes, and hopefully more."

As they rode along the road toward the farm, it occurred to Son that the villagers only knew part of the story. "Why didn't you tell them that the scouts were looking for me?" he asked.

Dulnear clenched his jaw and kept his gaze down the road. Taking a deep breath, he answered, "Because I would not want one of them to give you up to the slavers in exchange for an easy peace."

## CHAPTER FOUR

# A KNOCK AT THE DOOR

"Y ou did what?" Faymia gasped.

"We fought two slaver scouts," Dulnear repeated. "Or maybe they were bounty hunters," he added.

The four of them were once again sitting around the kitchen table picking at a soup Faymia had made while Son and the man from the north were in Laor. As the sky outside began to fade into shades of deep gray and shadow, Maren climbed partially onto the table and lit the lantern that sat as a centerpiece.

"And we warned the townspeople that more conflict is coming," Son added.

Faymia sat stunned as her husband and friend relayed the events of their trip into town. With each moment, any sense that there was time to prepare for battle faded. She stirred the contents of the bowl in front of her and asked, "Do you think they'll be able to fight?"

"Most assuredly not," Dulnear replied.

"What?!" the woman croaked.

The northerner pushed the corners of his mouth to one side and scratched at his cheek. "Well, at least not in their current condition," he explained. "But, we have a plan."

"We're going to train Henry," Son chimed in.

"The barkeep? You're joking!" Faymia sputtered. "He's more zeal than brains."

"That may be, but we do not have the luxury of seeking out the best candidates and auditioning for warrior-worthiness," Dulnear countered.

The woman didn't appreciate her husband's tone. However, she realized that his plan was better than no plan at all. "So, you're going to train Henry and release him to train the town?"

"That is correct," the man from the north answered.

For a moment, the room was silent as they pondered their predicament and sipped their soup.

"Someone's here," Maren half-whispered as she stared at an unusually large slice of carrot on her spoon.

Before anyone could ask how she knew, there was a knock at the door.

"That must be Henry himself," Dulnear announced as he sprang from his seat and jogged to the door. As he flung the door open, he was surprised to see someone other than Henry waiting on the other side.

"Hello, old friend," a deep voice came from outside. It was a fellow northerner. His large, fur-clad figure was imposing and dreadful. His head was wreathed in wavy blond hair that nearly covered his piercing blue eyes.

"Brunnlyn!" Dulnear shouted. "You are a sight for sore eyes."

"Please let me in," Brunnlyn replied. "That monstrous cat must have remembered me. It licked me, and now I smell like a rotting lobster."

"Is anyone else not going to finish their soup?" Brunnlyn asked. "It has been quite the journey." He had just finished eating what was left in the pot, and had polished off Faymia's leftovers as well.

"This one has giant carrots," Maren announced, sliding her bowl over to the man.

"Thank you, young maiden," the man smiled. He tipped the contents of the bowl into his mouth without the use of his spoon. Using his fur sleeve to wipe the broth from his bearded chin and mustache, he asked, "Are you sure that staying here is the smartest decision?"

Son sat and stared at the man for a moment. He then turned his eyes to Dulnear and Faymia, who also seemed to be waiting on him for an answer. "I don't know if it's the smartest or the wisest decision," he admitted. "But it seems like the right one. Ocmallum is a bully. He's a spoiled child of a man who's not used to being stood up to, so he's coming after the people who dared to push back."

Brunnlyn's eyes grew wider as the boy spoke. A small smile crept across his face. He asked, "So you think that you can defend yourself from the most powerful man in the south of Aun?"

Son breathed in deeply and exhaled. As he did, the northerner's question echoed in his mind. "No," he answered. "I cannot. But perhaps there's a chance with the help of my friends. Maybe, with their help, and the help of the Great Father, we can not only defend ourselves, but put an end to the slaver king's enterprise forever."

Brunnlyn's small smile now turned into a full grin. He leaned in and said, "If you would have declared it any other way, I would have told you to flee immediately. You have my sword, and the aid of the Saor."

Suddenly, a bloodcurdling scream could be heard from outside the cottage. It was followed by a monstrous roar.

Everyone around the table seemed to jolt upright in unison when they heard the noise, then Dulnear bounced to the door and flung it open. "Verrox!" he shouted. "Put him down!"

Son ran to the door to see what was happening. He could see that the giant cat had Henry by the boot and was swinging him back and forth. "Scratch behind her ear!" he called out. "She likes that!"

"And how am I supposed to do that?!" the barkeep called back as he was being tossed about like a rag doll.

Just then, his boot came off and he flew through the air, landing on his back. Dulnear ran out to help the man up, and the monstrous cat came bounding up to him with the man's boot.

"Verrox," the northerner drawled in a low voice. "Give me the boot."

The beast looked away as if she were ignoring the request.

"Verrox," he said more slowly and with greater sternness in his voice.

The animal dropped the man's boot to the ground,

faced Dulnear, and licked him across his bearded chin. She then trotted toward the barn and sat near its entrance.

The man from the north walked over to Henry with the wet boot, handed it to him, and helped him to his feet.

"W-what is that thing?" the barkeep asked, still trembling.

"That is a kottur," Dulnear answered matter-of-factly. "Sorry about the hole in your boot. Are you okay?"

"Y-yes," the man answered. He slipped his boot on while hopping toward the house. Once it was on, he continued to walk with a small limp as if a stone had found its way under his sock.

"Good," the northerner muttered. "She will be kinder to you after you are properly introduced."

"Hiya, Henry," Son greeted as he stepped aside to let the two men through the door. "I hope you're not hurt too badly."

"Hiya, Son," the barkeep returned, still visibly shaken from his encounter with the beast.

"She tried to eat me once," the boy added.

"Swell," the man grunted, and he looked around the table for a place to sit.

Once they were all seated, Dulnear asked, "Do you remember our friend Brunnlyn? He was with us when we returned from the slaver camp with Maren."

"Indeed I do," Henry replied. He cleared his throat and gained his composure. "Nice to see you again."

"I am sure," the northerner acknowledged. "Greetings."

"Well, it looks like we are all here," Dulnear began.

"Wait, this is it?" Henry choked. "The six of us are going to take on a slaver army?"

"Not quite," the man from the north explained. "For starters, you are going to train the townsfolk to fight."

"Even so, it's not going to be enough. Not even close!" Henry protested.

Son knew the man was right. Trying to assuage his fears, he announced, "I'll be traveling to Blackcloth to recruit some friends."

"Well, I hope your friends have an army," the barkeep blurted out.

"Wait, Blackcloth?" Maren chirped.

"Yes, I'm going to ask Aesef for help," the boy explained.

"And Phel?" the girl asked.

"If he's willing." Son answered.

"Oh, can I go?" Maren pleaded.

Son looked at Dulnear and Faymia to read their faces for approval or disapproval but found neither. "I guess so," he replied.

"Yesss," Maren whispered. "Phel."

Suddenly, Faymia broke in. "And I will travel to the Ohdium Rift to enlist the help of the chiefs."

There was a pause at the table as they all turned their eyes toward the woman.

"Perhaps that is a good idea," Dulnear considered. "But this time, I will be by your side."

"Actually," Brunnlyn interjected. "I was hoping you would join me."

Dulnear's eyebrows pushed down upon his dark eyes. Staring curiously at his fellow northerner, he asked, "Join you? For what?"

"We do not stand a chance as long as Ocmallum and his

men possess the borb," Brunnlyn began. "'Tis the berry we found when we fought the Greyus fighters on the way south from Tuas-arum."

"I remember," Dulnear murmured. "It was like they were possessed. I have never seen such aggression. What are you proposing?"

"I thought that the borb only grew in the far southern islands," he explained. "But the slavers have found a place on the The-as Peninsula where the conditions are ripe. They have built a plantation there."

Dulnear swallowed hard. Clenching his left hand into a fist he declared, "Then you and I must burn it down before they can harvest it for the attack."

"That is my proposal," Brunnlyn said.

Dulnear looked at his wife and tilted his head. "My darling, will you be okay without me?"

Faymia closed her eyes for a moment, then held her gaze with her husband. "Storming a plantation sounds like a job for a warrior such as yourself," she sighed. "The chiefs of the Ohdium invited me to call on them should the need ever arise. I'm sure I'll be fine."

The room was quiet as the friends contemplated their future actions. Son could feel anxiety grow as he considered Dulnear's and Faymia's plans.

Breaking the silence, Henry asked, "And what about me? How will I get trained?"

"One of my Saor brethren will be along to train you," Brunnlyn promised. "We have days, not weeks, before the slavers are here. I suggest that we prepare right away and leave at first light."

Son looked around the table. His palms were damp and

he felt the room move around him. He wanted to suggest that they say a prayer but his mouth was dry and he lacked the words. "Okay," he muttered. "First light."

CHAPTER FIVE

# SEPARATE WAYS

As Son rode his horse north toward Blackcloth, he wondered if all of their efforts would be enough. Perhaps running and hiding would have been a better decision for the safety of his friends. Maren sat behind him with her hands on his waist. Occasionally, she would twist and turn to see landmarks they had ridden past, and she had to be reminded to sit still.

"How much further?" the girl asked.

Son had answered this same question several times already and it was still morning. Trying not to sound exasperated, he answered, "We should arrive sometime before dinner."

"Will Phel be there?" she asked.

Once again, the boy tried to keep a kind demeanor in his voice. "You've already asked me that," he said. "I really don't know the answer, but I have no reason to believe that he won't be there."

"Okay," Maren sung. She then began to tell herself a

story about the surrounding countryside and its propensity to harbor bandits and other unsavories.

Son was accustomed to her habit of softly telling herself tales, and her voice seemed to fade into the distance as he further pondered their situation.

Mostly thinking out loud to himself, he asked, "Where can we find more people to fight with us?"

The young girl tapped her chin and shoved her mouth to the side. "Hmmm," she hummed. "Doesn't your father live in Blackcloth?"

Maren's question felt like a shove to the cold ground. Son had thought about his father many times since he last saw him. They were not particularly fond thoughts, but there was a lingering hope that one day they could put their differences aside and enjoy each others' company. "My father?" he blurted. "I don't think he'd want to help me."

"Why not?" Maren asked. "He should want to protect you. Any father would."

Son allowed himself to imagine fighting side by side with the man he had always seen as strong and capable. He dreamed that perhaps the conflict he found himself in with the slavers would be enough for the man to endear himself to his son, and they would mend the wounds of the past. Taking a deep breath, he exhaled, "All right, we'll make a stop at my uncle's before going to see Aesef."

***

It was a long ride into Blackcloth. A fading sky hung over the bustling city streets and an acrid smell rose up to meet it. As Son's horse trotted toward his uncle Kione's house, the boy noticed how tired and shabby the people looked.

The last time he was in the city, he discovered that his mother had passed away, and that his father had abandoned him to claim her estate. It was then that he said goodbye to the man for the final time. At least he thought it was the final time. He never thought life would bring him back to this place, or to the man who wounded him like no other.

"I don't know if I should do this," he called back to Maren.

"Okay," was the only counsel the young girl offered.

They approached a row of semi-detached houses on the northern side of the street. In the middle of those houses was his uncle Kione's residence. It was the dingiest of the lot and, if not for the light of a lantern burning inside, it could easily have been mistaken for an abandoned dwelling.

Many of the unpleasant feelings that plagued Son during his last visit began to soak into his heart as if the events had happened yesterday. The sorrow of losing his mother and the anger and pain of his father's abandonment seemed to momentarily rob him of his courage and confidence as a warrior. He could feel his heartbeat through his entire body as he approached the house.

"Maybe it will be different," he said. "Surely, he'll see my predicament, feel bad for how he treated me, and stand with me now."

"I'll say a prayer," Maren offered, and Son could hear her whisper something from behind his back.

The boy rode as close to the door as he could, hopped off his horse, and handed the reins back to Maren. "Wait here," he instructed. "I'll be as quick as I can, and hopefully we'll have another ally against the slavers."

"Okay," Maren sang, and she held the reins with a slight grin.

Son knocked on the door of the house. His stomach felt strange, and he could hear his pulse throbbing in his right ear. There came a shuffling from the other side of the door. He imagined it to be his father, and wondered how he would respond to seeing his boy grown into a young man, able and strong.

The door opened slowly. On the other side of it stood an aging, bloated, bald man. "What do you want?" the man grunted.

"Hello, Uncle Kione," the boy said politely.

"Who are you?" the man asked as his eyes moved over the lad.

"It's me. I'm your nephew, Son."

Kione's eyes grew large and he ran his shaky hand along the top of his smooth head. "Well, I'll be," he exclaimed. "Look how big you've grown. Come in, come in."

Son stepped through the doorway into the house. It looked much the same as it did the last time he was there. A desk sat against the staircase to the left, and a small table and chairs to the right. The kitchen sat behind the front room, and the boy could see piled dishes and filth growing on its countertops.

Before Son had a chance to state the intention for his visit, his uncle observed, "You sure do look like him."

"Look like who?" the boy asked.

"Your father," the man answered plainly.

Feeling an unusual sense of pride for bearing a resemblance to his father, Son asked, "Where is he? I was hoping to speak to him."

"You mean you haven't heard?" Kione asked.

"Heard what?"

"Your father passed away months ago," his uncle explained.

The words seemed to be spoken from a distance, and echoed through Son's ears like a voice in a dream. He felt the need to sit down but stayed on his feet for fear that he would not be able to stand again if he rested. "Died? But how?" he stuttered.

"His heart just gave out," Kione said. "I guess all of his hard living just caught up with him."

A stampede of wishes immediately trampled over Son's mind. Wishes that he would have implored his father to drink less, wishes that he would have returned sooner, and wishes that everything would have been different about their relationship. "I can't believe it," was all he could mutter.

"I'm sorry to be the one delivering the sad news," his uncle said. Then, after pausing for a moment, he added, "I suppose you want to know about the will then."

"A will?" the boy blurted out. "I guess I'm surprised he even had one."

"That makes two of us," the man admitted. He then turned toward the desk beside the stairs and began rifling through some papers. "Here it is. A bit strange, since he didn't have much. Even the farm belonged to a relative that was kind enough to let him live there."

Son stared intently at his uncle. His face was hot and his legs were weak. "What does it say?" he asked.

Kione studied the document with a stern expression. It was only two paragraphs long and carried a sloppy signature at the bottom of it. "Well, let's see here... being of sound mind... etcetera, etcetera... no part of my estate is to go to my son for reasons that are personal to me and known to him."

Like a spear through Son's chest, the words of his father's will tore through him. His eyes burned and he could barely suppress the heaving in his chest. "For reasons that are personal to me and known to him? What was he talking about?"

"I don't know," Kione admitted. "I'm not even sure he knew."

"So, my father passes away, and his very last act on earth is to strike at me!" the boy lamented.

"I'm sorry," his uncle tried to comfort. He turned and placed the will back on the desk. As he did, he scratched his chin in thought. "I have a couple things of his. Not much. A shirt, and a pipe, and a couple of odds and ends. Would you like them?"

Son sighed. "I thought I wasn't supposed to receive anything that was his."

"Well, he left them in my house," Kione stated. "That makes them mine to do with as I please, even if it means giving them to you."

"Thank you," the boy said. "I will take them."

As the man slowly climbed up the stairs, Son studied the old house. Amidst its cluttered, deteriorating state, memories came to him, both good and bad. He could almost feel his father's presence there, and the feeling that he would never see him again weighed heavily on his shoulders.

"Here it is," his uncle called down, and he began to descend the staircase with a burlap sack.

Son reached out to take the sack. As he did, he noticed how heavy it was. "What's in it?" he asked.

"Not much," Kione confessed. "Like I said, a shirt and a pipe. There's also a small wooden box that your father used to keep tobacco in." He then scratched at his temple and added, "And maybe a leather belt. That old bag has been up there for a long time and, to be honest, I don't really know."

"Okay," Son breathed. "Thanks again."

The two stood in silence for a moment until Kione invited, "Well, would you like to sit down for a tea?"

Son remembered that Maren was waiting outside for him. He knew it would soon be dark and felt an urgency to get out of the city so he could set up camp. "Thank you for the invitation, but I really must be going."

"Okay, boy," his uncle said. "It was good to see you again. I wish it was under happier circumstances."

"Me too," Son agreed. He gave a sad smile to Kione, turned, and exited toward the street.

Son rushed to find firewood before it was too dark to see the ground. He would have gone straight away to Aesef's farm but, when the sun went down, the pitch-dark night sky in Aun made it unsafe to travel. They had found a flat patch of ground a stone's throw from the road and hitched the horse to a tree.

"I made a circle with rocks," Maren called out from the clearing.

"Thanks," the boy called back. "Please gather some small twigs that we can use for tinder. I'm just about done fetching wood."

Moments after returning to the clearing, Son had a small fire burning, and they sat beside it nibbling on small oaty cakes of nuts and dried berries they had made for their journey. When they were finished, Maren took out a book and moved closer to the fire so she could read it.

As Son sat in silence, he remembered something. "My father's belongings," he said out loud, and he fetched them from his horse's saddlebag. As he stood near the animal, he asked, "Did you feed Capall?"

"Uh-huh," the girl replied without looking away from her pages.

The boy took the burlap sack his uncle had given him and returned to the large, smooth stone he had been using for a stool near the fire. Placing the bag on the ground between his feet, he opened it. As he did, the smell of his father came rushing into his nostrils, causing memories of good and bad times to play through his mind with alarming clarity. Though it was mostly the odor of sweat, ale, and cigarettes, he took it in fondly and, for a moment, it felt as if his father was nearby.

He let out a deep sigh and his chest began to heave. He couldn't understand how he could feel such a deep loss for a father who seemed to care so little for him. The sense of sorrow melted into the agony of the words of his father's will, and the combined anguish threatened to squeeze the very life from his broken heart.

Soon, Son began to sob. Tears ran down his face and his body trembled until he could no longer hold onto the bag. He rested his elbows on his knees and wept into his hands. He mourned a friendship that never was, words of love that were never spoken, and a future that would never be. The orphaned ragamuffin from Blackcloth would never find the happy ending with his father that he longed for.

As he continued to grieve, he felt a small hand on his shoulder. He knew it was Maren offering him some comfort. He reached a shaky hand upward and touched hers.

"I'm sorry," she said softly.

Son couldn't find the words to respond, but her gesture brought him a small amount of relief.

"I never thanked you," the girl continued.

The boy dragged his sleeve across his upper lip. Turning red, swollen eyes toward his friend, he asked, "Thanked me for what?"

"When you first found me on the road, my mother and father had just been crushed," she explained. "You didn't hesitate to take me into your care, even though Dulnear discouraged you."

Son swallowed and wiped his face once more. "You're so very welcome," he struggled to say. "You are my family now, and taking you with us was one of the best decisions I've ever made."

Maren wrapped her arms around the boy's neck and squeezed tightly. Kissing him on the cheek, she declared, "I love you, Son."

"And I love you," the boy returned, and began to sob afresh.

After he had cried out all his tears, Son noticed that Maren was still standing with her hand on his shoulder. He turned and wrapped his arms around her. "And thank you," he said. "I have learned so much about life, and joy, and determination from you."

"Uh-huh," the girl replied with lips pushed to the side, and she sat down on the stone next to the boy.

After the two had sat staring into the fire for a while, Maren asked, "Um, may I see what's in your bag?"

Son was reluctant at first. It was the only thing he had that belonged to his father. Eventually, he slid the bag over to her and said, "Sure, but please be careful."

"Okay," Maren murmured. She reached into the bag and pulled out a shirt. Sniffing the item, she wrinkled her nose and set it aside. Pulling out the old wooden tobacco box, she asked, "What's this?"

"I think my father kept his leaf for smoking in there," the boy explained.

Maren opened the box and wrinkled her nose once more. "Smells like burning leaves," she complained. She then pointed to a small, tubular object in the box and asked, "What's this?"

"Oh, that's a pipe for smoking," Son said, and he picked it up and examined it closely.

Besides a few bits of dried tobacco, there was nothing left in the container. The young girl held it out with her left hand and scratched her head with her right. Squinting, she asked, "Why is it so heavy?"

"I don't know," the boy replied, still studying the old wooden pipe in his hand.

Maren grasped the box with both hands and gave it a shake. She then set it on her knees upside down and stared intently at the bottom of it. Giving it a thump with her fist, she asked, "Did you hear that?"

"Hear what?" Son asked, turning his attention to the box.

Giving it a couple more knocks, she exclaimed, "There's something in there. This box has a false bottom!" She then grabbed a stone from the ground and began to pound on the bottom of the container.

"No, wait! You'll break it!" he protested.

But before Son could stop her, the wooden slat that formed the bottom of the box had broken in two, and the source of the sound that Maren had heard became exposed.

"There were gold coins wedged in there!" the girl declared. "They must be worth thousands!"

Son could hardly believe what he was seeing. He snatched the box and completely removed the broken board. "Eight coins, to be exact," he muttered. "I didn't think he had anything."

"Are you going to keep them?" Maren asked.

Son thought for a moment. "The will said that I was to receive no part of his estate… " He rubbed his chin and stared into the dancing flames before him. "But this was lawfully my uncle's, and he gave it to me, so I suppose that it still honors the will to keep it."

Maren made a dancing motion with her feet and giggled.

"What's so funny?" Son asked.

"Your father thought he had the last word in an argument you didn't even know you were having."

"And?"

"The Great Father had another idea."

"I suppose he did," the boy laughed. "I suppose he did."

## CHAPTER SIX

# AESEF

Son and Maren rode the long trail to Aesef's, the boy recalling their last trip there, when thugs had attacked, leading to a violent confrontation.

Son was thankful for the graciousness of the old farmer, and hoped that his hospitality hadn't waned since they last spoke.

After arriving and hitching their horse, Maren ran ahead and excitedly began knocking at the door.

"Wait for me!" the boy cried out, but before he could reach her, someone was already opening the door.

"Phel!" Maren shouted when she saw the face of the lanky, fair-skinned man in the doorway.

"Maren?" the man sang. "Is that you?"

"Uh-huh!" she answered. "And Son!"

"Oh my goodness!" Phel shouted as he reached down to hug the girl's neck. "You've both grown so much!"

As Son approached the doorway, he reached for the man's hand and shook it vigorously. "It's great to see you!"

"And great to see you, lad," the servant proclaimed.

"Come in. You must be exhausted from your journey. I'll let Aesef know that you're here."

Phel brought the two travelers through the large entryway, down a short, broad hallway, and sat them next to each other at a large wooden dining table. After fetching them both a cup of cold water, he ran off to bring in their friend.

It wasn't long before a broad, sturdily built, white-haired man appeared from the kitchen. His wild, white beard was contrasted by his tan, rough skin, and he seemed to have the energy of a dozen horses. "It's really you!" he shouted, and he ran up behind them to embrace both of their necks at once. "What brings you all this way?"

"Um," Son said sheepishly. "I wish it was because I had happy news. Can you spare some time?"

"Of course!" the man declared. He then whispered something to Phel, sending him out of the room, and sat down across the table from his old friends.

"So, the last time we were here, we had to deal with thugs trying to prove their manhood with fire and steel," Son began.

"I remember," Aesef shuddered. "They almost burned the place down."

"Well, a while back, Maren... " the boy said, then trailed off for a moment. He wanted to explain their predicament, but didn't want to embarrass the girl. "She, uh, was tricked into becoming a slave."

The old farmer's eyes grew wide and the wrinkles in his forehead shot upward. "No!" he mouthed.

"Yes," Son blurted. "We broke her out of a slaver encampment and brought her home."

Aesef exhaled for what seemed an impossibly long time.

"I'm really sorry to hear that. You know they're not going to just let that go."

"I know," the boy lamented. "And, on the journey to find Maren, I had a run-in with Ocmallum himself."

"What?! You met the slaver king?" the farmer choked.

"Met him? I broke into his house and bested him with my sword," Son confessed.

Aesef's face turned pale-white. He leaned back in his chair and covered his mouth in shock. "Son," he gasped. "I don't know how you're still alive."

"I'm only alive because they haven't found me yet," Son clarified. "But Ocmallum has had bounty hunters all over Aun looking for me. We ran into some just outside of Ahmcathare, and then again in Laor just before coming here."

The old farmer's back shot up straight. "In Laor?? It's only a matter of time before they're on your doorstep at Gale Hill!"

"That's why we're here," the young warrior said. He paused for a moment and thought through his words carefully. "I know that, if we hide, we will hide for the rest of our lives. But, if we stay and fight, we have a chance to put an end to the slaver king, and slavery in all of Aun. It's just that we need help." He then leaned in toward his friend and asked, "Will you join us in our fight?"

Aesef looked as if a rock had fallen on his head. He stared blankly at Son, and the boy began to wonder if he had somehow offended the old man.

"I, um... " the farmer hesitated.

Just then, Phel came bursting into the room. "Sir!" he shouted. "There are men outside brandishing swords!"

Aesef stood straight up. His eyes darted back and forth between Son and Maren. "Not again!" he sputtered.

"What do you want?" Aesef called out from the doorway.

The afternoon was gray, and tiny drops of rain were falling lightly to the ground.

Five men formed a semicircle within spitting distance of the house. Each of them held out a sword that looked as worn and haggard as they did.

"Just give us the boy and the girl, and we'll be on our way," the man in the center of the semicircle instructed.

Aesef stepped outside. He was holding a sword almost as long as he was tall. "Are you men bounty hunters?" he asked.

"We're just folks aiming to collect some coins," the same man replied. "Every slaver in Aun is offering a year's wage for those two."

Son felt a familiar shiver as he heard the man's words. He held tightly to Maren's hand as she tried to see around Aesef to get a better look at the men. He was about to ask Phel to take her someplace safe but the man was nowhere to be seen.

"I think you all should forget that they're here, and leave," the farmer announced. He held out his sword with both hands clutching its hilt. "It would be a pity if you were injured, or worse."

The five thugs seemed amused by the old man's threat. "We're not afraid of a fat old farmer!" one of the men called out.

Son released Maren's hand and stepped out to stand next to Aesef. Surprisingly, Maren did the same, and now they each stood on either side of the man. The boy withdrew his sword, took a deep breath and replied, "That old farmer is my friend, and you should do as he says."

"Not without you and the rugrat!" the goon in the middle shouted. His lip began to twitch and his face seemed to gradually be turning a light shade of red.

Son ran through his memories to try and visualize what Dulnear would do in a situation like this. His mentor was so much more physically imposing than he was, which the boy believed was the key to his confidence. Though he was shorter than average, and far less intimidating, he tried to dispirit the men anyway. "I'm afraid you're going away empty-handed today," he began. "And if you insist on staying, it will be to your dismay."

*Not bad*, the boy thought to himself. *That should rattle their cages.*

The boy's thoughts were suddenly interrupted when the gaggle of bandits erupted with laughter. "Is that supposed to be scary?" one of them called out. "I saw a dead raccoon on the side of the road that was more frightening!"

"Dead raccoon," Maren whispered with a giggle.

"It's okay," Aesef said quietly. "We can work on some better taunts later." He then winked at the boy before focusing his eyes back on the thugs.

"Does this mean that you're coming to Laor?" Son quietly asked the farmer while holding his gaze on the men.

"I'm leaning that way," the farmer confessed. "But first, we need to get rid of these vagrants."

"Thanks for the laugh!" the man in the center of the

semicircle cackled. "Now, I'm going to count to ten. If you're not over here by the time I'm finished, then I guess we'll have to settle for the smaller bounty for bringing you back dead."

Aesef took his right hand off his sword and placed it on Son's shoulder. "Don't be afraid," he consoled. "I've got this."

Something about the bounty hunter's threat seemed to create a gritty urgency in the boy. Hearing the news that he could be brought to Ocmallum dead angered him, rather than scared him. It was a response he wasn't expecting, but he was strangely pleased with it all the same. His nostrils flared as he filled his lungs with air. "No, *I've* got this," he declared.

Maren cleared her throat and stepped forward, waving a rolling pin from the kitchen. "No, *I've* got this," she chimed in.

"Hey, how'd you get my rolling pin?" Aesef asked.

Instead of answering, the young girl charged forward at the man in the center of the semicircle. She was followed closely behind by Son, who was yelling something about waiting up and not being foolish.

The leader of the pack of thugs chuckled as he saw the girl moving closer. However, his laughter quickly turned to cries of agony as she dropped to her knees and repeatedly hammered his shin in rapid succession. He dropped hard onto his side, clutching his leg, and ordered, "Kill her!"

The man to Son's right thrust his sword directly toward the boy's neck, which he blocked swiftly with an outward motion, then brought his sword down onto the man's ankle, and back up to his temple. The cut cleaved off the top of the man's ear and left a gash next to his eye.

"You little bastard!" the man shouted as he dropped his sword and rummaged through the tall grass for the top of his ear.

Son was about to give the man a swift kick to the ribs when he noticed a third man dashing toward him. He planted his right foot behind him and stood in a fighting stance.

Suddenly, Aesef came running by with his sword, ready to strike the man. He slashed downward on the bandit's right shoulder, almost cleaving it from his body. The man dropped to the ground, rolled onto his stomach, and began to crawl away using his legs and one good arm.

When Son saw that the man was no longer a threat, he turned his attention back toward Maren, who was holding her own against her opponent. He was now fighting her while perched on his knees. Why Maren didn't just take a few steps back and avoid the thug altogether, Son didn't know. He noticed two of the men move toward the kneeling man to assist him, so he ran over to fight next to the girl.

The men grunted out some garbled threats which the boy paid no heed to. He was going to say something snide, but had decided that fighting banter just wasn't his strength, and felt it best to focus his attention on swordplay so he could eliminate the threat of the hooligans.

Recalling Dulnear's lessons on fighting multiple attackers, he took Maren's arm, stepped back a few paces, and drew the men into a single line in front of their assumed leader. This would keep the men from surrounding him, and allow him and Maren to double their efforts upon one man at a time.

As the first man raised his sword to attack, Son prepared to block and retaliate. But before their swords had a chance to meet, there was a *whoosh*, then a *thunk, thunk, thunk*, and all three men were on the ground clutching arrows from various locations on their bodies.

"Hey, thanks for lining them up for me like that!" Phel called out. He was standing on the roof of the house with a bow and a quiver full of arrows. "Great idea!"

Son was confused for a moment, then yelled back, "Thanks! Glad I could help!"

"Nice shooting!" Aesef shouted to his servant. He wiped the blood from his sword and walked over to the boy and his young ward. "Well, you two sure have grown as fighters," he complimented.

"Uh-huh!" Maren smiled.

The farmer then looked at Son sternly. "Phel and I will join you," he began. "And I'll see if I can recruit any of my farmhands. But, for now, please take Maren back into the house. I need to have a word alone with these gentlemen."

Son took a deep breath and did as he was told. He felt a sense of relief that the farmer was joining them, but certain realities of violence and bloodshed were adding heaviness to his decision to take on Ocmallum.

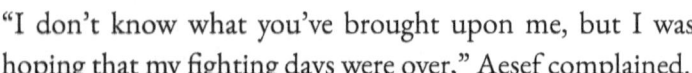

"I don't know what you've brought upon me, but I was hoping that my fighting days were over," Aesef complained.

"I am sorry," Son apologized. "I had no idea that we

were followed here, or that we'd be fighting goons in your garden."

The old farmer took a deep breath. His forehead wrinkled and he massaged his temples. As he exhaled, his face softened. He murmured, "We're going to have to teach you to recognize when you're being tracked, and how to move about without leaving hints of your whereabouts." He then added, "I'm surprised Dulnear hasn't taught you that."

Son didn't know what to say, so he just added another, "I'm sorry."

Just then, Phel came in through the front door and entered the dining room where they were seated. Leaning a dirty shovel against the wall, he announced to Aesef, "All set."

"Where?" the farmer asked.

"Back in the field that we left fallow this season," Phel answered in a slightly hushed tone.

Son shuddered at the thought of burying bodies, and the casual manner in which it was discussed. "I'm sorry," he said for a third time. "I didn't mean to bring trouble here."

Aesef leaned across the table and locked eyes with the boy. Son could tell the man was carefully considering his words before speaking. "We don't always get to choose who, or what, comes into our lives, or the consequences they bring," he began. "But what we choose to do about it can form us into greatness. Son, I believe that you are going to be a great man one day."

Son was relieved and encouraged by the man's words. "Thank you," he gushed. "I suppose Maren and I better be heading back to Laor now."

"Not without eating first," Aesef insisted. "There is stew in the kitchen, and bread made just this morning."

"And jam?" Maren chirped.

"And jam," the farmer laughed. "After lunch, I'll head off with you. That way, I can show you how to avoid being tracked in the future. Phel will stay behind to see how many of the workers he can recruit, then join us as soon as they can."

"Okay, that sounds good," Son breathed. He leaned back in his chair, looking forward to a warm meal. As he did, he wondered how Dulnear and Faymia were faring on their journeys.

CHAPTER SEVEN

# THE RIFT

Faymia urged her horse across the countryside. She rode through field and farmland, avoiding roads and well-worn paths for fear of encountering a slaver blockade. It made the journey to the Ohdium Rift much slower, but the last thing she wanted was to draw attention to herself.

It was difficult for her to tell how near she was to her destination because she had only ever approached the rift from the east-westerly road before. She continued east, trying to find any familiar landmarks, but as the sky turned from light to dark gray, her searching became more difficult. Eventually, she found a cluster of trees settled within a field of tall, golden grass and decided to camp there for the night.

Without building a fire, she tied her horse to a nearby tree, leaned against a fallen oak, and covered herself with a blanket. When she was settled, she ate one of the oaty cakes Son had prepared for her before his departure. As she gazed out across the rolling field, trying to acclimate her eyes to the growing darkness, it dawned on her that this was the first time she had been by herself for a significant amount of time. At least for as long as she could remember. There was no Maren to look after, no Dulnear to lean against, and no Tcharron to belittle or demean her. The silence was both comforting and unsettling at the same time.

She had begun to wish that she had built a fire while there was enough light to do so. Her small meal was gone, the air around her was pitch-black, and the hunger and darkness seemed to amplify the unsettling nature of her solitude.

Faymia wiggled her way down onto her back from her position against the tree. The ground was unforgiving and cold, and she tried to get as much blanket as possible between herself and the ground without becoming uncovered. She laid on her side and stared out into the blackness with a sigh.

She hoped that Son's decision was the right one. Having been a slave herself, she knew how the slavers refused to let go of even the slightest of offenses. They would deploy any amount of resources to show the rest of Aun that they would not be disrespected, even to their own detriment.

She took a deep breath of the cold night air and closed her eyes. As she did, she let her thoughts drift toward her husband. She still couldn't believe that he had spent his inheritance to purchase her from Tcharron. The thought filled her with gratitude, and she smiled. Hoping to get through her meeting with the Ohdium chiefs quickly, and return to her love, she mentally rehearsed what she was going to say to them until sleep overtook her.

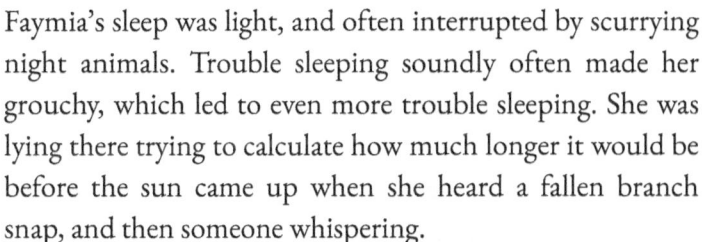

Faymia's sleep was light, and often interrupted by scurrying night animals. Trouble sleeping soundly often made her grouchy, which led to even more trouble sleeping. She was lying there trying to calculate how much longer it would be before the sun came up when she heard a fallen branch snap, and then someone whispering.

The woman's eyes shot open and she listened carefully to gauge which direction the voices were coming from. It was difficult because her own startled heartbeat was throbbing in her ears and making it difficult to hear.

"Around here someplace," one of the voices said.

"How can you tell? We can't see a thing," another voice whispered.

"There's no one out here. Let's go back," a third voice pleaded.

Faymia slowly reached for the sword she had laid near the top of her head. Praying that her horse remained silent, she held her breath, hoping the men would pass on by without noticing her.

"This is ridiculous," one of the voices said quietly.

"I know I saw someone out here," another said, sounding agitated.

"Shhhh! You'll tip them off," the other warned.

Faymia remembered her first night in the Ohdium with Maren. It was a terrifying ambush as she was accused of being a spy for the Taalbrem lowgrounders. But the Rift was supposedly in unity now.

There was the sound of another branch breaking, and an "Owww!"

"Be careful!" a voice chided in the darkness.

"That tears it! I'm lighting a torch and heading back!" the other voice exclaimed.

The sound of steel hitting rock could be heard. Then there were several sparks, and a burning torch was raised in the air. It lit up the area by the cluster of trees, and Faymia could see that there were indeed three men, and they were much closer than she had initially thought they were.

"A horse!" one of the men cried out.

Faymia jumped to her feet with her sword at the ready. Saying nothing, she waited for them to make their move.

"And a woman!" another man declared. "A one-eyed woman!"

All three men fixed their eyes on Faymia. The two men without torches withdrew their swords and stood ready to fight.

The man with the flame called out, "Identify yourself at once, or face our wrath!"

Faymia took a step closer. "I've encountered greater wrath from a litter of kittens," she jabbed. "I am Faymia of Laor. Who are you?"

"We are guards of Le'as. Chief of the Taalbrem," one of the sword-wielding men answered. "And you are trespassing."

The woman sighed with relief. "You mean I'm at the Ohdium?" she asked.

"Of course," the same man answered. "These are the grasslands west of the low ground village."

"Of course!" Faymia exclaimed. "I should have known."

"Well, state your business," the torch-carrying man demanded. "Or we'll put you in the dungeon."

Faymia chuckled. "I've already had my share of Ohdium dungeons. Just take me to your chief. I need to see him."

"Take me to your chief? Just who do you think you are?" the same man queried.

"Wait a minute!" the other armed man burst out. "That's her!"

"That's who?" his comrades asked.

"That's the lady with the eyepatch. The one who persuaded the chiefs to talk. She brought the rift back together!"

"At your service," Faymia smiled. She let her shoulders relax and sheathed her sword.

The guards did the same, and the man with the torch drew closer. "What are you doing out here?" he asked. "It's not safe these days."

"What do you mean?" she asked.

"Strange men snooping around," he explained. "They look like they were pulled out of the dung heap and given old swords. From far away, we thought you might be one of them."

Faymia felt her lip twitch as she heard those words. "Bounty hunters," she said. "They're the reason I'm here. I must speak to Le'as and Thuaid immediately."

"We'll lead you back to the chief's chambers," the man said. Glancing back at his companions, he added, "I'm sure he will be pleased to see you."

Faymia rushed to stow her blanket in her horse's saddle-bag. "I sure hope so," she murmured. "I need to ask him a big favor."

The sky gradually changed from black to dark gray as Faymia and the three guards reached the house of Le'as. It sat in the center of the sleeping village square without any light coming from its windows.

The man carrying the torch knocked at the door and waited for an answer. "He's probably still sleeping at this time," he explained. "I'll give it another rap."

There was a glow from inside that got brighter as it moved closer to the window. The sound of a bolt being slid from its catch could be heard. The door creaked open and a muscular man with a white beard stood there staring strangely at the visitors.

"Sir, this woman insists on speaking with you at once. She claims it is most urgent," the chief's guard explained.

The man at the door cocked his head sideways and stared for a moment. "Faymia?"

"Le'as, I need your help," she blurted. "Can we talk?"

"I'm surprised to see you! Of course, come in!" he invited.

Faymia entered the chief's house, followed by the three guards.

"Let me light some lanterns and put something on besides this robe," Le'as said. "And I'll wake the servants to get some breakfast on. Please have a seat near the fireplace."

As Faymia's eyes adjusted, she could see that there had been some redecorating since her last visit. The inside of the house took on a grander appearance. Near the fireplace sat four large leather chairs. She wasn't sure which one to sit on so she chose the one that would be warmest once the fire was lit. When the man with the torch lit the fire, the flames grew and the cold night dampness began to dry from her clothes. She was glad for her decision to sit where she did.

The woman could hear some bustling in the kitchen and the house seemed to gradually fill with the buzz of people rushing around to provide light and prepare breakfast.

The man with the torch put out its flame and rested it on the hearth. He then sat next to Faymia as the other two stayed standing behind the two vacant chairs.

"I'm Jarmour," he announced.

"Pleased to meet you," Faymia smiled, though her only concern was speaking with Le'as.

"You probably don't remember me, but I was there the day you defeated Soeth," he said.

"Oh, that terrible woman who tried to kill my friend and me," Faymia recalled.

"I always knew that treasonous shrew was up to something," Jarmour confessed. "I only wish I had the boldness you did to call it out."

Faymia took a deep breath and let her shoulders relax. "Thank you," she said. "That is very kind of you to say."

Before the guard could get out another word, Le'as was seated across from the woman, looking intently into her eye. "Now, what brings the uniter of the Ohdium to my door at such an early hour?" he asked.

"Sir," she began. "These guards have explained to me that you have had strange men lurking about the rift lately."

The chief's eyebrows shot up and his neck cocked back. "Indeed we have. Do you have insight into their motivations?"

"I'm afraid I do," Faymia began. "I'm sure you remember my young friend, Maren."

"Why, of course. One does not easily forget such a unique child," he smiled.

"Well, she was deceived into slavery some time back." The woman paused to choose her words carefully. "And my friends and I did what we believed was necessary to set her free."

Le'as let his mouth drop open as he listened to the story. He leaned in even closer as his hand reached upward to cover his lips.

"During our conflict, Son, the boy who was with my husband, bested the slaver king in physical combat, leaving the man in humiliation."

"Say no more!" the chief interrupted. "Ocmallum is now unleashing his resources to make a demonstration of the boy, and anyone who assists him."

Faymia went silent for a moment and drew a deep breath. "That is correct," she nodded. "Those shabby men you've seen are most likely bounty hunters searching for us. They somehow knew we were here before, and are hoping we'll return."

Le'as leaned back further into his chair. He repeatedly opened and closed his fists as he stared wide-eyed at the woman. "Lady Faymia, I had no idea you had such powerful enemies. We can try to hide you among the blessed ones above the cliff, but that is no guarantee of safety for you and yours."

"Thank you, sir," the woman answered. "But hiding is not our plan. We aim to put an end to the scourge of Ocmallum, and I'm asking for you to fight alongside us."

As the words tumbled out of Faymia's mouth, she could hardly believe she was saying them. Her hands shook, and her legs felt weak.

The chief's wide eyes narrowed and he scratched the side of his head. His face turned pale. "You're asking us to go to war against the most powerful man in Aun with you? I don't even know how to answer that."

Faymia felt her eye grow warm and she stifled a tear. "I know that is a tremendous ask," she began. "And, if you say no, I will understand. I'm only appealing as one who believes that doing nothing will only assist men like the slaver king in placing our land under oppression and exploitation."

Le'as shook his head. "You really cannot ignore it when things aren't set right, can you?"

"To a fault," she answered squarely.

"Okay," the chief exhaled. "Even though we've never had slavers in the Ohdium, I agree that Aun would be a much better place without them." He hesitated for a moment as he looked into the fire. "And you have been a true friend to my people. I will consider mustering forces to help." He then looked back up at Faymia. "But only if Thuaid agrees. We are one people once again, and I won't make that decision alone. Jarmour will take our fastest horse and retrieve the highground chief."

Faymia had finished her breakfast quickly and returned to her chair by the fire to wait for Jarmour to return with the highground chief. Le'as sat across from her and assured her that his guard would return quickly.

"Forgive my impatience," the woman apologized. "I'm desperate to return to my friends before Ocmallum finds them."

"I understand," the chief sympathized. "But, if what you say about bounty hunters is true, then taking plenty of time to start heading back might be wiser since they'll be watching."

Faymia sighed, knowing that Le'as spoke the truth. "Thank you for that," she said. "I will try not to let my desperation hamper my judgement."

No sooner had she spoken those words than the door flung open and Thuaid came bounding in with his aide Argach. Trailing behind them was Jarmour, out of breath from trying to keep up.

"Faymia!" the highground chief shouted, and he ran over to embrace her before she could fully stand to her feet. "Jarmour filled us in. The answer is yes, whatever you need." He then paused and looked at Le'as. "That is, if my lowground counterpart is willing."

Argach also gave his greeting to the woman, and he, the two chiefs, and Faymia sat down in unison to discuss the goings-on that brought them together that morning.

"I know that what I beseech is dangerous," Faymia explained. "I risked much to keep the two of you from going to war, and now I'm asking you to fight alongside me." She stopped speaking for a moment and examined both of the chief's faces. A sense of disbelief settled over her. Surely she was not sitting in a royal chamber recruiting an army to battle the most powerful man known to her. She took a breath and continued. "But more hangs in the balance than just the safety of my friends. This could end the trade of slaves in Aun for good."

Thuaid leaned into the woman's words, sitting forward in his seat.

Le'as, however, sat back and rubbed the palms of his hands against the arms of his chair. He stared at the ceiling, then addressed her. "I agree that slavery needs to end. And I am for fighting," he began. "But it is already against the law to force the people into it. They must go willingly. Even though they are lured by pleasures and false promises, they still make that choice. Won't they just find their way into another form of bondage?"

A sense of shame attempted to burrow its way into Faymia's heart as she heard the words spoken. She recalled her own journey into slavery, and the love of her husband that purchased her freedom. "That may be true," she said. "In fact, I was once a slave."

There was an audible gasp in the room as Faymia made her confession. Her ears rang with the new silence that settled over her surroundings, and she could feel the judgement aimed at her as if it were an arrow ready to be released. It was by sheer will that she continued speaking.

"But we're all susceptible to a slavery of one sort or another," she said. She thought hard about her words as she continued. "When I first came to the rift, the two of you were slaves to bitterness and anger. You were willing to risk the peace of your people and go to war over grievances trumped up by dishonest men."

Both chiefs glanced at each other, then back at Faymia.

Their faces told her that they had no words, and any air of self-righteousness had disappeared.

"But you had a choice," she continued. "You could have released yourself from your bondage at any time. And you did once you learned the error of your ways. I didn't have that luxury. There was no rehabilitation for me. I realized my mistake the first time my slaver struck me in the face and locked me in a cage. I couldn't change my mind. My captivity didn't come with a chance to repent and return to my life before. Not until Dulnear used his family inheritance to purchase me and give me my freedom. It was a gesture never before seen in Aun, and is unlikely to be seen again."

Le'as now leaned forward in his chair as well. His eyes were red and his lips pursed. "I apologize. I did not mean to offend," he murmured.

"It's understandable," Faymia answered. "Those who have not sunk to such dark places often falsely believe they have the answer for those who have. And those who have, rarely find a way out without the help of those who haven't."

Le'as nodded and gave an awkward smile. He glanced toward the highground chief, then back at Faymia. "Well, I am in agreement with Thuaid," he announced. "What can we do?"

Faymia felt a sense of lightness drift over her as she heard the man's words. Moving to the front of her chair, she exclaimed, "Rally together as many fighters as you can, and meet me at Gale Hill posthaste."

"You have our word," Thuaid broke in. "As a deposit, take Argach with you while we gather troops. If Lady

Faymia says we can make our land better, then I'm behind it."

"Indeed," Le'as agreed. "Take Jarmour with you as well. The three of you will have a much better chance of making it back to Laor in safety."

As the two chiefs' aides nodded toward Faymia, she began to plot her journey home, and hoped that Dulnear would be returning soon as well. She was about to announce her departure when Le'as spoke.

"You should wait until the very first inklings of light tomorrow morning," the man advised. "It would be wise to travel when visibility is lowest, but not pitch-dark, and take to the fields as you did when you came."

"I agree," Thuaid chimed in, rubbing his bearded chin.

The woman was feeling impatient, but she knew the men were speaking wisely. She nodded at the two of them, and slid fully back into her chair.

"We will have provisions and weapons gathered for you and your trek home. Argach and Jarmour will gather what they need as well," Le'as explained.

"And we will assemble as many able-bodied soldiers as we can, and follow shortly after," Thuaid added.

Faymia thanked the two men for agreeing to join her. For the rest of the day, they made plans for travel, and for defending Gale Hill when the time came.

CHAPTER EIGHT

# THE MEETING OF THE SAOR

D ulnear and Brunnlyn rode over long-neglected trails and obscure paths that scarcely resembled roads. Winding and twisting through wooded fields and farms, they made their way north and east with the intent of traveling around Dorcadas, then heading south to the The-as Peninsula.

"I do not need to remind you of how dangerous this is," Brunnlyn called to Dulnear.

Dulnear was deep in thought and hardly heard his friend speaking to him. He finally noticed a stream running along the left side of the trail and shouted back, "I think it would be a good time to water the horses." He then tugged at the reins of his horse and the beast slowed down.

When Brunnlyn had caught up with him, they both dismounted and led their animals to the stream.

Dulnear's thoughts were on Faymia. The world around him seemed pale and distant as he imagined how she was faring on her mission to the Ohdium. "I pray that our efforts are not mere futility," he thought out loud.

"That makes two of us," his countryman agreed.

"We are wasting valuable time avoiding the main roads," Dulnear added. "It may be more expedient to take a direct approach and battle anyone who gets in our way."

Brunnlyn smiled in amusement at Dulnear's words. "I know that stealth is not a northerner's preference," he began. "But if Ocmallum catches wind of two northerners moving in the direction of his plantation, he will surely fortify his defenses, and set a trap for us there."

"I suppose you are right," the man from the north agreed. "I reckon that he is marshaling his army of goons at his estate in Dorcadas. I wish the boy would have killed him when he had the chance."

Brunnlyn wrinkled his forehead, and looked deep into his friend's eyes. "Do not wish for Son's youthful compassion to fade too quickly," he admonished. "Life will take it from him soon enough."

Dulnear sighed. "I know you are correct. He has my heart, and is very dear to me. It is only that... "

"That he attracts as much trouble as a northerner?" Brunnlyn chuckled.

Dulnear smiled. "Truth!" he laughed. "Maybe that is why I see so much of myself in him."

"And what else?" his friend asked.

"What do you mean?"

"What else is distracting you?"

Dulnear felt embarrassed. All day, his mind had been conjuring images of Faymia suffering, injured, or worse. "I am worried for my wife," he confessed.

"That is reasonable," Brunnlyn assured. "But there is nothing you can do for her at the moment, and leaving half of your heart with her means there is less of you available here and now, where we both need all of you."

The man from the north paused and considered his countryman's words. He patted the side of his horse's long, muscular neck. "Thank you for the reminder," he murmured. "I will do my best to keep my focus present."

Brunnlyn stepped closer to his fellow northerner. Placing his hand on his shoulder, he stated, "Brother, I cannot promise that we will prevail. But I will hold nothing back to see you and your friends to victory. I swear my life on it."

Dulnear was moved by his friend's devotion and placed his hand on Brunnlyn's shoulder as if he meant to embrace him. "I apologize," he began. "Though Faymia is the dearest creature in the world to me, I vow to keep my mind present. If not, I fear that you and I will both be worse off for it."

Brunnlyn nodded gratefully, then stepped back to take hold of his horse's bridle. "We will be reaching the edge of Dorcadas soon," he announced. "We need to proceed with caution."

"That dreary little hamlet," Dulnear spit out. "Perhaps we should go directly to Ocmallum's estate and burn it to the ground."

"That would be quite the feat for two left-handed men. Let us put our focus on the plantation," his friend replied.

Dulnear nodded and prepared to mount his horse, but the idea of a preemptive strike on the slaver king took root in his mind, and he wondered if it could be done.

"Just a little further," Brunnlyn announced.

They had been riding all day. They rode a wide arc north around Dorcadas and were now to the east of the village. They halted their horses and, in the waning evening light, Dulnear could see an open, rolling field with a cluster of immense oaks at its center. For the first time all day, he realized that his left hand was cold and his nose was dripping from the chill in the air. He fetched a handkerchief from the pocket of his fur coat and wiped his nostrils.

"There," his friend chirped, and he pointed to the grouping of oak trees. "That is where one of our Saor brothers will meet us."

Dulnear nodded and gently prodded his steed across the field. He felt it was odd that other men from the north held him in such high regard and had allowed their right hands to be taken in order to mitigate the legacy of violence in Tuas-arum.

When they arrived at the foot of the trees, Dulnear was impressed by their enormity. He led his horse under the canopy of their giant limbs and tied it to a low branch. Gazing upward, he asked, "Have you been here before?"

"Many times," his friend answered. "I hid here when I first left the north. Not once, in the long while that I camped here, did I see hide or hair of anyone else until Onclaid found me."

"Onclaid? I know that name," Dulnear muttered.

"You should," Brunnlyn said. "We were in school together."

"Right, angry fella. Even for a northerner, he was mad."

"Well, he was the first to lay down his malicious ways and join me," Brunnlyn explained.

"Unbelievable," Dulnear exclaimed. "It is difficult to believe that there is a fellowship like the Saor."

"I agree, and I lead them," Brunnlyn chuckled. "But you started it all."

"Be that as it may, I still cannot believe it," Dulnear repeated.

The two warriors hastily put together a camp, barely getting a fire lit before the sky turned black, squelching their ability to forage or hunt. Sitting on a massive fallen tree trunk, they stared into the flames, saying little until Dulnear spread out his bedroll next to the trunk and reclined on the ground.

"Sleep well, my friend," Brunnlyn said. "Hopefully, we will be resting here again tomorrow night after destroying the enemy's borb crop."

"Hopefully," Dulnear murmured. He laid on his right side, facing the fire and his companion. With his hand resting on the hilt of his sword, he said a prayer for Faymia and Son.

The smell of lamb stew filled Dulnear's nostrils and the sound of laughter filled his ears. In his dream, he was home again seated at the kitchen table with Faymia, Son, and Maren. Each of them were sharing stories of adventure and victory, and the cloud of Aun's slavers was no longer over their heads.

Amidst the joyous revelry, he stared into the face of his beloved wife, and his heart was filled with such affection toward her that a tear escaped his eye.

"Is that a tear I see?" Faymia asked with a tender smile.

Slightly embarrassed, the man from the north wiped his cheek and began to explain, "Maybe," he said. "It is just that I... "

Dulnear found himself trailing off, unable to speak in that moment. He could not find the words to express his immense love and gratitude for the remarkable woman sitting before him. As he searched his very full heart, a sudden strange darkness filled the room.

The man's keen senses pulled him from his dream. He sat up with eyes moving quickly through his pitch-black surroundings.

In the far distance, the warrior could see a faint light moving slowly through the rolling field. He got up from the ground, sat on the fallen log, and kept his hand on his sword.

"Brunnlyn," he whispered. "Rouse yourself. Someone is approaching."

"That must be Onclaid," his friend answered. "He is running ahead of schedule." Shaking the cobwebs from his head, he shuffled over and took a seat next to Dulnear.

As the torchlight came nearer to the cluster of oak trees, it picked up speed. The man from the north could barely make out the shape of another northerner riding horseback. He relaxed his grip upon his sword and exhaled. "It is a strange time of night for travel," he observed.

A stone's throw from the campsite, the rider dismounted his horse and began to run toward Dulnear and Brunnlyn. As he did, he withdrew his sword and growled.

"I do not think that is Onclaid," Dulnear announced.

"Not if he can hold a torch and sword at the same time," Brunnlyn agreed.

The two men bounced to their feet and held their swords at the ready. The strange northerner tossed his torch at their feet, then slashed his sword downward toward Dulnear's left shoulder.

Dulnear stepped right, narrowly missing the blade, and almost knocked his friend backward over the log they were previously sitting on. He quickly stepped behind the log to make space between himself and the attacker. Brunnlyn did the same.

For a moment, the three men stood and peered at each other through the faint, flickering firelight. In that moment, Dulnear noticed that the man was the largest of the three of them.

"Where do you come from?" Dulnear called out.

"Ifreann!" the man bellowed in a chilling low voice.

Ifreann was northern-speak for Hell. Dulnear was not amused by the man's answer. Broadening his shoulders and chest, he replied. "If it is games you wish to play, then so be it. But know that it is we who make the rules here, not you."

A gravely laughter emitted from the attacker. "Oh, the mighty Dulnear and his famous banter. I have waited a long time for this."

Surprised by what the man said, Dulnear nearly dropped his sword. Before he could say another word, the intruder hopped onto the fallen tree trunk and was using both hands to bring his sword down, hard and fast.

This time, Brunnlyn struck down the attacker's blade with his sword, but the stranger retaliated with a fierce kick, sending Brunnlyn backward until he lost his footing and fell to the ground.

The man leaped from the log with his arm drawn back to plunge his sword into Brunnlyn, but Dulnear swiped hard in an outward arc, not cutting the man, but knocking him off his trajectory so he missed his target.

Brunnlyn bounced back to his feet and stood ready. "I suppose you have tracked us down to collect a bounty," he deduced.

The stranger turned his gaze onto Brunnlyn for a moment. With a wicked grin, he rasped, "I do not know who you are, Nairetu, but I am sure that Ocmallum would not hold it against me if I returned with two heads in my saddlebag."

As the man addressed Brunnlyn, Dulnear lurched forward with his sword, piercing the man's fur coat, puncturing his side. The man spun around like a wounded fox and swung his blade toward Dulnear's neck, nearly taking off his head.

Brunnlyn pressed in on the other side, and the attacker managed to stave off both northerners as they sped up the pace of their deadly dance around the fallen tree.

Like fur-clad cyclones, they battled until the black sky turned into a charcoal gray. Dulnear was growing weary, and his mind sought for ways to put an end to the battle. He maneuvered his way between the log and his assailant with the intent to kick the still-burning torch into the man's face, causing him to involuntarily raise his arms to block it. This would give him a brief opportunity to plunge his sword into his ribcage.

But before Dulnear had a chance to execute his plan, he

misjudged the location of the fallen log and tripped over it, falling backward.

"Clumsy lummox!" the immense, dark northerner barked.

As the world became dimly lit, Dulnear could see that the man was a Mai-ru. They were a tribe of men from far north of the Petraig Mountains. They lacked the refinement of those south of the mountains, and some legends say that the violent northern temperament originated from that region. He had many braids in his long black hair, and his fur looked like it was torn from a rotting kottur.

Dulnear rolled to his feet before the man could attack again. "It does not surprise me that a Mai-ru would attempt to slay his countryman for money!" he yelled. "It is dogs like you that bring shame to our people."

"Spare me the self-righteous lecture!" the stranger returned. "You have never lacked anything, and it is now time for me to receive my comeuppance!"

Suddenly, a massive blade emerged from the man's chest. He looked down at it in horror and confusion, then went limp. As the sword retreated from his body, he fell to the ground, and another northerner stood in his place.

"Onclaid!" Brunnlyn shouted. "You are right on time!"

"I see that you had an uninvited guest," the man observed as he wiped the blood from his sword on the Mai-ru's fur coat. Then, turning his attention to Dulnear, he introduced himself. "I do not know if you remember me from our learning days, but I am Onclaid, son of Senclaid."

"Of course," Dulnear replied. He was impressed by the man's ability to sneak up on his victim, and made a mental note to not turn his back on him. "Thank you for dispensing with our morning irritation."

"I am at your service," Onclaid chimed. "The Saor owe you a debt of gratitude."

"That remains to be seen," Dulnear said with a smirk. "We have all sacrificed our right hands to end cycles of violence, but have only been drawn into new ones."

"What news do you bring?" Brunnlyn asked as he stepped forward to where the other two were standing.

"Well, for starters, Ocmallum has Mai-ru in his employ," the man said. "But I reckon you have already deduced that."

"Indeed," Dulnear groaned. "But what of the borb?"

"I have scouted the plantation on the The-as Peninsula," Onclaid began. "It sits on the jagged shoreline, and is fortified by a wall similar to the one around Ocmallum's estate."

"And what of the harvest?" Dulnear inquired.

"'Tis a bumper crop this season," Onclaid explained. "They must be planning on supplying berries for all of their gang. It is stored in silos just inside the plantation walls."

"What about security?" Brunnlyn asked.

"Mostly locals," the Saor brethren said. "The slaver king is amassing quite an army at his estate, which means that his other interests are being run by hired hands and mercenaries."

"Good!" Dulnear grinned. "Then we can make quick work of those rabble and rob the slavers of their precious borb."

"Possibly," Onclaid muttered.

"What do you mean by that?" Dulnear asked.

"I mean that it may not be as easy as it sounds. Some of these hired hands are Greyus fighters, and you know their affinity for ingesting these berries, and how difficult they can be to stop."

"I remember," Dulnear stated. "Aggressive little toads."

Dulnear rubbed his chin in thought. His memory of dealing with the Greyus along the road to find Faymia wasn't pleasant. However, he knew that the borb had to be destroyed if they stood a chance against Ocmallum. "How long of a journey is it from here?" he asked.

"If we leave now, we can arrive just before dusk," Onclaid explained.

"Good!" Dulnear exclaimed. "Will you be joining us?"

"If that is what you wish," the man answered.

"Excellent! Is your steed nearby?"

"At the bottom of the hill."

"Then let us make haste!"

The three northerners quickly gathered their things and mounted their horses. As they began to move south, Dulnear hoped his plan would work, and that he would soon be on his way back to Gale Hill to reunite with Faymia.

## CHAPTER NINE

# FIELD OF BLOOD

Faymia, Argach, and Jarmour rode west across field and farmland toward Laor and Gale Hill Farm. The woman was tired and anxious, but glad to have company on her return journey.

At midday, they stopped to water their horses at a stream that seemed to be much too weak and small for the bed it ran through. As Faymia dismounted, she glanced around to make sure no one else was nearby. They were further south than the route she had taken the day before. It gave her some comfort to be further away from the road, but the land felt foreign, and their path unsure.

"There is a strangeness about this place," Argach observed. "Are we getting closer to your farm?"

"I think so," Faymia answered, though she was not as certain about her answer as she wanted to be.

Jarmour stretched his back as his horse drank from the stream. Gazing at his surroundings, he admitted, "This is the farthest I've ever been from the rift." He then added, "I imagined there to be more cities."

Faymia chuckled at the man's sheltered perspective. "There are many cities outside of the Ohdium," she explained. "Magnificent cities."

Argach joined the woman in her amusement. "Have you really never been outside the rift?" he asked.

Jarmour's cheeks turned red as he pressed his lips together and shook his head back and forth.

"Thuaid sends me to Ahmcathare quite regularly on errands," Argach explained. "It's a magnificent place."

Faymia winced upon hearing the name of the great city. Her time spent as a slave there was something she wanted to purge from her memory. As she recalled her experience, she noticed a small group of men riding from the north, across the field toward them.

"Are those slavers?" Jarmour asked.

"I don't know," Faymia answered. "But we'd best be on our guard."

The woman could hear her heartbeat grow louder in her ears as she watched the group travel closer. She contemplated fleeing, but was wary of revealing the direction of their destination. She reckoned that her best option would be to force the group to play their hand first.

She held out her bow, nocked an arrow, and instructed, "Arm yourselves. We will see what they want. Perhaps the battle begins today."

The men drew nearer, and halted their horses. There were five of them, each armed with pitchforks and butcher knives. "Identify yourselves!" one of the men called out.

"Only weary travelers passing through," Faymia answered curtly with her arrow squarely aimed at the man.

The men stared through squinted eyes and furrowed

brows, and occasionally glanced at one another. Their prolonged silence made Faymia uneasy.

"Now, you identify yourselves," the woman demanded, keeping her bow trained on the man nearest her.

"We own the land you've been riding through," the nearest man said. "There have been strangers snooping around our places. Rumor has it, they're bounty hunters looking for a boy, a young girl, a northerner... and a one-eyed woman."

Faymia shuddered to hear herself mentioned that way. She swallowed and asked, "And when did you see these strangers last?"

"Just this morning," the man answered. "We chased them off, and thought you might be them returning."

Faymia felt her shoulders relax as the man told his story. She lowered her bow and replied, "I'm terribly glad to hear that. You have probably guessed by my eyepatch that I am the woman they're looking for."

Suddenly, a knife came hurling through the air, embedding itself into the woman's left shoulder.

"That's her! Get her!" the man called out, and the riders behind him urged their horses toward the travelers.

Faymia reached over with her right hand and dislodged the knife. She then turned her bow on the nearest rider. Releasing her arrow, it sunk deep into the man's neck. Grasping for it, he fell hard onto the ground as his horse came to a sudden stop.

Argach and Jarmour stepped out in front of Faymia to protect her as three more riders continued to charge.

Two of the men on horseback rode to attack from the left while the third peeled off to attack from the right.

"I'll take this one!" Faymia declared as she stepped forward and aimed her bow at the solitary rider. Meanwhile, Argach and Jarmour ran out to meet the other two.

As the deceitful bounty hunter charged with pitchfork extended, Faymia released her arrow, striking his arm. She watched as the sudden surge of pain caused him to jerk the horse's reins. The animal then reared high on its hind legs, tossing its rider to the ground.

Faymia was terribly disappointed with herself for lowering her guard and allowing herself to be vulnerable to attack. She turned toward her companions, who were doing their best to fend off attacks from the other two bounty hunters. Seeing that Jarmour's attacker was about to take another pass at him, she fired an arrow, sinking it into the man's thigh, causing him to fall from his horse as well.

She was about to pull another arrow when she felt something blunt strike her back, sending ripples of pain down both her legs. Spinning around, she saw the man she had previously struck while charging her. With her arrow still lodged in his right arm, he held a crudely carved club in his left hand.

He swung for Faymia's temple. Unconsciously, she raised her right hand to block. Unfortunately, she was holding the bow in her right hand, and the hoodlum knocked the weapon to the ground.

The woman rolled to her left and planted her left foot firmly behind her as she took a dagger from her belt and held the blade firmly against her forearm.

"You're lucky Ocmallum wants you alive," the thug muttered.

"And you're lucky I missed your chest," Faymia

quipped as she glanced at her arrow sticking out from both sides of his arm.

The man snarled and lunged at Faymia with his club. As he did, she ducked then rose and backhanded the man with her left hand.

Instantaneously, he threw his left elbow at her, striking her on the temple.

Faymia clenched her teeth and willed herself to maintain her focus though she could feel dizziness try to come upon her. As she stepped back, she punched the man squarely in the jaw with her knife-wielding right hand. He took a step back and countered with his right fist. The action was clumsy since he was bleeding freely from the arrow impaling his arm.

The woman blocked with her left hand, then reached forward to grab ahold of her arrow and wrenched it from the man's forearm. Howling in pain, he sputtered out curse words between groans and stumbled backward.

"I'll kill you for that!" he bellowed.

"I've heard it all before," Faymia replied as she returned to her fighting stance, planning her moment to put an end to the melee.

The bounty hunter ran toward her, swinging his club wildly. Faymia managed to step out of the way and dodge each swing, which seemed to enrage the man. She managed to land another blow against his jaw but instead of sending him backward, it only seemed to make him angrier. He drew his club back for another swing and as he did, she punched her arrow into his ribcage.

Looking down at the arrow, the man curled his upper lip and muttered more garbled threats. He came at her again, swinging his baton. This time, Faymia fell to one knee and quickly plunged her knife into his upper thigh and dragged it downward toward his knee before pulling it out.

The man released his weapon and dropped to the ground, reeling in pain. As he did, the woman stood up and stepped backward. "Are we done?" she asked matter-of-factly.

In reply, the man only groaned from the ground, shoving his hands onto his freshly gushing wound.

Faymia looked over to her companions, who seemed to have accomplished similar outcomes with their opponents. She then turned her eyes northward, looking for the man who was leading the group, but he was gone. "Where did he go?" she called out to Argach and Jarmour.

"I didn't even see him leave," Jarmour answered.

"This doesn't bode well," Argach added. "I suggest we ride hard and try our best to leave a difficult trail to track."

Faymia did her best to suppress thoughts of panic. She could only imagine what fresh torment the man would bring with him when she saw him again.

CHAPTER TEN

# THE BORB

The three northerners crouched in the dense woods near the borb plantation. The ground was covered in dead pine needles, and the trees looked gaunt and sickly. All that could be heard was the sound of flies buzzing in thick swarms nearby. Dulnear was concerned that the woods were not enough to provide adequate camouflage, and did his best to remain low to the ground as they surveyed the massive walls around their target.

"This is madness," Brunnlyn lamented.

Dulnear did not disagree with his friend. However, he tried to be a bit more optimistic. "All great conquests are considered mad until after they are accomplished," he encouraged. Turning his attention toward Onclaid, he asked, "What lies beyond the seaside wall?"

"It is a sheer drop to the rocks below," he said. "There is not so much as a ledge to stand on."

"So, cliffs to the west, and the incoming trail from the east," Dulnear thought out loud.

"There are guards posted all around the wall," Brunnlyn observed.

"'Tis just like Ocmallum's estate," Dulnear muttered.

"How did you manage?" Brunnlyn asked.

"We almost lost our lives, and only the guards in Ocmallum's inner sanctum had the borb," Dulnear explained.

As the man from the north continued to survey the plantation from the forest, he felt a stinging sensation on his neck. "That must be the fifth biting fly to feast upon me," he observed.

"I have been bitten several times as well," Onclaid said in a half-whisper.

"They must enjoy northerners," Brunnlyn added. "I have lost count of the number of flies I have killed."

"It is as if the very air here is a putrid draw to these pests. I suppose these are the conditions in which the borb thrives," Dulnear surmised.

"This is going to be a difficult task if we are going to be eaten alive," Onclaid complained.

Dulnear exhaled through his nose. It was as if the biting flies were growing worse as they sat there, and they now seemed to be forming thick clouds in the air closer to them. "They must be drawn to the berries," he stated. "This whole place is detestable."

"What do you suppose we do?" Brunnlyn asked.

Dulnear rubbed his chin. His eyes squinted as he thought. Suddenly, his eyebrow shot up as he recalled, "My mother used to plant wild catnip around our garden. There was some growing in the woods where we just tied the horses. We must gather as much of it as we can."

Brunnlyn chuckled, "'Tis not the time to think of your enormous beast. What is your plan?"

"It will repel the flies, and most other bugs, from this forsaken place," Dulnear explained.

"I trust what you say," his friend replied. "Let us head back to the horses before it gets too dark."

When the three found their horses in the woods, they noticed that the air was clear and they were no longer being bitten by flies.

"Just what I thought," Dulnear began. "There is catnip everywhere in this part of the woods. Gather as much as you can. Stuff your pockets with it, rub it on your hands and face, and do not use it sparingly."

The three northerners plucked as much of the plant as they could from the ground, stuffing it in their pockets, under the collars of their coats, and even creating head-bands out of twine and catnip.

"You both look terrific," Onclaid joked.

"Take comfort in knowing that you look just as ridiculous," Dulnear retorted. "Now, let us return to the edge of the woods and test my theory."

When the companions returned to their earlier positions, Dulnear was pleased to see that the flies no longer bit him, or would even land on him. Sighing with relief, he stated, "Now we can attack without the distraction of biting flies from the hellish pit."

"What is your plan?" Brunnlyn asked eagerly.

"'Tis simple," Dulnear answered. "The two of you will attack from the south side, drawing their defenses toward you. I will sneak in from the north side and set the berries ablaze."

Brunnlyn winced when hearing the plan. "The two of us will be outnumbered by borb-crazed warriors. I am confident we can take out a few, like we did on the road to Laor, but there will be no margin for surprises."

Dulnear looked up in thought, then suggested, "What if the two of you apply stealth, taking out guards until you reach the center of the borb field? By the time you announce your presence, I will be inside with you ready to set the field ablaze. Once it is lit, I can join you and we can fight our way to the exit."

"It gives me only a minuscule amount of comfort, but I suppose it is the best plan we are going to come up with between now and nighttime," Brunnlyn murmured.

Dulnear closed his eyes and took a deep breath. He was not used to having his plans questioned, but wisdom told him that his own counsel may not be enough. Tilting his head, he asked, "How can we make this plan better, my friend?"

Brunnlyn squinted until his eyes could barely be seen. Scratching the back of his head, he answered, "The borb makes these men aggressive beyond reason. Why not use that against them?"

Dulnear pushed his mouth to one side, and his mind reached for ways to do as his friend suggested. Then, it dawned on him and a smile crept across his face. "You mean to get them to battle each other."

"Indeed," Brunnlyn chuckled. "Onclaid and I will take out the guards on the wall, sneak down into the courtyard, and get the rest to fight each other. You should be able to slip in and set your fire unnoticed, and the two of us will not even need to draw our swords."

"Oh, I like that," Dulnear laughed. "You are brilliant."

"The ideas just come to me," Brunnlyn joked.

"This is going to be fun," Onclaid added.

The sky was dark, and if not for the torchlight coming from within the compound, the three northerners would not be able to see a thing. Dulnear watched Brunnlyn climb to the top of the wall and crouch in the shadows as he waited for the nearest guard to pass.

The man from the north was pleased with their plan, but he still suspected there was an even chance for success or failure. He wondered how Onclaid was doing at the north side of the wall.

"Wait for my signal," Brunnlyn called down in a heavy whisper. He then slit the throat of the passing guard and tossed his body off the wall, with it nearly landing on Dulnear.

Dulnear looked down at the dead Greyus warrior, disgusted by its sickly appearance. *One down*, he mused, and he fixed his eyes back onto his friend as he waited for the signal to pass through the gate and set the borb ablaze.

Brunnlyn kept low as he moved along the wall silently eliminating the guards. He paused and scanned the north wall and noticed that there were fewer guards now pacing the top of it. *Well done, Onclaid*, he thought to himself. *I hope you brought plenty of stones.*

When he noticed another guard approaching, he laid on his back and quietly rolled himself toward the inner part of the wall where it was darkest. The guard stopped a mere hand's width in front of Brunnlyn and sniffed the air. As he did, his shoulders drooped and he shook his head as if waking up from a dream. Popping to his feet, Brunnlyn wrapped his right arm around the man's neck, and quickly stabbed his knife into his temple with his left. He then tossed the body off the wall to join the others.

The northern warrior crouched back into the darkness and scratched his head as he looked around. *Why is this not more difficult?* he thought to himself. *Perhaps these are not the same Greyus. Or maybe the berries have lost their potency.*

When the northerner had cleared the watchmen from the southern wall, he surveyed the western wall and noticed that there were no guards along it. He reckoned it was most likely because there was only a sheer cliff drop below it. Gazing to the east, he saw that the east wall was empty as well. However, the lookout towers on either side of the gate were each occupied by one guard. Suppressing any sense of suspicion, he focused on the plan and waited for Onclaid to indicate that he was ready.

When he saw his fellow northerner standing at the center of the north wall waving, he knew it was time to move onto the next phase of their plan. He turned toward the outer ledge of the wall and signaled down to Dulnear that it was time for him to go into the courtyard.

Dulnear stood with his back against the eastern wall and slowly slid toward the portcullis gate that entered into the courtyard. He hoped his confrontation with the guards would be quick and quiet, and not alert the tower watchmen.

A small amount of light shone from inside, its orange glow dancing through the gate, projecting a strange waltzing display on the ground.

The man from the north took a stone from his pocket and tossed it just a little ways out past the light. When one of the guards stepped out into the darkness to investigate, he slipped in next to the remaining guard and quietly eliminated him.

"It was nothing," the investigating guard called out as he returned to his post. He then glanced to his right for a moment and sniffed the air. "Do you smell that?" he asked.

Dulnear realized that the darkness on the north side of the gate was sufficient to hide his presence from the guard. He stepped toward the man and asked, "Smell what?"

Before the man could react, the man from the north slammed his head into the wall behind him, rendering him a limp shell that he tossed into the outer darkness with the other guard.

He then quietly hefted the portcullis high enough for him to get through, and crept through the gateway to the courtyard. Once on the other side, he noticed that most of the interior of the compound was composed of rows of berry bushes that grew up just past his waist. Walking the perimeter, and up and down the rows, were fast-moving Greyus guards, occasionally plucking berries and shoving them into their mouths like starved jackals.

Dulnear observed them with disdain at their craving for the borb, then turned his attention toward the silhouette of Brunnlyn, who was hunched down atop the southern wall. Taking another stone from his pocket, he hurled it up toward the man, striking his shoulder.

*Not bad for a left-handed throw*, he thought to himself, and he froze in place as he waited for his friend to move.

Brunnlyn quickly stood to his feet, took aim with a rock of his own, and managed to bean one of the guards along the inside of the northern wall.

The sound of a snort, and a "Who did that?!" sputtered from the man. He pounded his chest and turned his gaze toward the guards along the southern wall.

Suddenly, one of Onclaid's stones pelted one of the guards along the southern wall, and the man gushed forth with obscenities. "Someone wants to die!" the man screeched.

Brunnlyn followed up with another stone, striking a different guard this time. As predicted, he withdrew his sword and threatened, "You fools are going to eat my blade if you do that again!"

Onclaid then tossed another stone, and it was followed by another of Brunnlyn's, and this continued until the Greyus on each side of the courtyard were standing toe-to-toe, wagging weapons in each other's faces.

Then, the inevitable happened. One of the guards on the northern side plunged his sword into the belly of a guard on the southern side.

There was an eruption of metal and flesh as the two sides clashed. Like rabid dogs, they attacked each other until there weren't even two sides anymore. There were only crazed men hacking at each other until they had bled too much or lost too many limbs to continue.

Dulnear watched in equal parts horror and relief. When the guards seemed to be at the zenith of their frenzy, he ran back to the eastern wall to retrieve one of the torches that were mounted there.

Reaching for a torch, he felt a sudden pain in his left shoulder. Spinning around quickly, he was confronted by two Greyus warriors standing before him. *The tower guards*, he thought. *Great*. Trying to ignore the dagger protruding from his shoulder, he drew his sword.

The guards said nothing, but followed suit with their own blades and lurched forward.

The man from the north stepped left and slashed inward. As he did so, he knocked the torch to the ground, singeing his coat as it fell.

The guard to his right ran forward with savage speed and mirrored Dulnear's inward attack, but he was blocked by the northerner's massive blade, then kicked backward by an equally impressive boot. In the blink of an eye, the hostile tower guard was back on his feet resuming his attack.

Dulnear felt another surge of pain in his shoulder and realized that the man to his left had run behind him, pulled the knife from his shoulder, and was now attempting to lodge it into his ribs. He threw his arm backward, striking the man with the hilt of his sword, then smashed the other guard with a steel fist to the face. Before the man could close the distance again, he swung his sword downward, taking off the man's leg.

The man fell to the ground but continued without a

leg as his borb-fueled assault continued. Appalled by the sight of the one-legged tower guard clawing along the ground toward him, Dulnear took a step backward, forcing his back against the courtyard wall. As he did, a strange, smokey mint odor filled his nostrils, and he realized that his coat had caught fire from the torch on the ground.

From his left, the uninjured tower guard came charging. "Hold this," Dulnear jeered, and plunged his sword completely through the man's abdomen, leaving it there while he quickly removed his burning fur coat.

Seeing the other guard quickly crawling toward him, he tossed his smoldering coat on top of the man, then retrieved his sword from the innards of the impaled guard, who immediately dropped to his knees with a quizzical expression on his filthy face.

Suddenly, a terrible cry of agony rang out from under Dulnear's coat. "My leg!" the man wailed. "You cut off my leg!"

"Huh?" the man from the north grunted. He used his sword to lift his jacket off the man, who now seemed to be void of the aggression and savagery that filled him only moments earlier.

"You stupid lummox! I'll get you for this!" the guard threatened as he held his hands over what was left of his blood-gushing leg.

Confused, Dulnear asked, "I am sorry. Did your precious berry lose its potency?"

"I just ate them!" the man shouted. As he did, a crazed look overcame him and he grabbed onto the northerner's boot.

"Wait a minute!" Dulnear exclaimed as he kicked the man back. It then occurred to him. "The catnip!"

He reached over with his sword and flicked his smoking coat back onto the guard, and instantly the man reeled in pain once again. Dulnear laughed at his discovery, then lifted his coat from the man's face. "So, smelling the catnip takes some of the aggression off, and breathing in its smoke makes you downright pathetic," he taunted. He then flung his coat back to the ground, grabbed the man by his only leg, and flung him into the rows of borb, where he was quickly consumed in the ongoing melee between the other guards.

Dulnear then stomped out the remaining flames of his coat and put its charred remains back on. "As for you," he said to the other guard who had been reduced to a pale, weak, clawing creature. "You may have your last meal." He pulled a small amount of smoking catnip from his pocket, took to one knee, and shoved it into the man's mouth. Seconds later, the man gurgled his last breath and his body went limp.

Giving thought to his discovery, Dulnear nearly forgot that he was there to set the plantation ablaze. He stepped back, grabbed the fallen torch, and quickly moved along the ends of the rows of borb, setting them on fire. When he saw that the flames were spreading toward the other end of the courtyard, he tossed the torch into a patch of berries that hadn't caught fire yet and ran back toward the portcullis gate.

He lifted the gate enough to get underneath it, then turned, expecting to see a swarm of Greyus men running to join him. When he peered through the gate, he was astonished. Not only were there no warriors running to escape the flames, but the ones who remained continued to fight each other like frenzied animals.

Dulnear's stomach turned as he witnessed the senseless slaughter. "Unbelievable," he said to himself.

"What is unbelievable?" a voice asked from the darkness behind him.

The man from the north spun around with his hand on his sword, but relaxed when he saw that it was his companions, Brunnlyn and Onclaid.

"That went better than I had expected," Onclaid admitted.

"Brunnlyn is quite the genius," Dulnear agreed.

The three of them stood in the near-darkness for a while, recounting the experience from their own perspective. As they did, the fire from inside the compound walls began to fade, and the clashing of metal grew silent.

"This victory should be a relief to your friends in Laor," Brunnlyn stated.

Dulnear thought about what the man had said. He knew they needed to return to Gale Hill Farm immediately, but wondered if there was anything else he could do to even the odds before returning. "Indeed," he said, then rubbed his chin in thought.

"Something is on your mind," Brunnlyn observed.

"Perhaps we can leverage this blow to Ocmallum for an even greater advantage," Dulnear pondered out loud.

Brunnlyn tilted his head to the side and eyed his friend

suspiciously. "Is it wise to take unnecessary risks while the town waits for our return?"

"Oh, I do not believe there will be much risk involved, so long as we hurry," Dulnear explained. He then turned toward Onclaid and instructed, "Retrieve a torch for us so we can find our way back to the horses." He then walked over to the bodies of the two outer gate guards and beheaded one of them. Picking the head up by the long, stringy black hair, he explained, "We shall leave a message for the slaver king at his own front door. Perhaps it will demoralize his troops. After all, a battle is often won or lost before it even begins."

Brunnlyn shook his head and pursed his lips. "You may be right," he agreed. "But you are an insane *gealt*."

Dulnear chuckled at the use of the northern-speak term for lunatic. "Perhaps I am," he said. "But saneness never changed the world."

## CHAPTER ELEVEN
# THE MESSAGE

"What is your plan?" Brunnlyn asked as they stood in the woods outside the slaver king's castle walls. The dull morning light was just beginning to turn the sky from black to the darkest of gray.

"I will attach a note to this head and toss it over the wall," Dulnear answered.

"And then what?" Onclaid inquired.

"Then we run as they shriek like goats," Dulnear chortled.

Brunnlyn squinted and scratched the side of his face. "So you are telling me that we came all this way to perform a childish prank?"

Dulnear considered the man's assessment of his idea. He then defended it. "I do not know any children who have tossed a human head over a wall. They will cry out in terror, and reconsider their allegiance to Ocmallum."

"I hope you are right," his friend murmured.

"Do not worry," the man from the north murmured in return.

The three men crept closer to the wall closest to the courtyard. Dulnear remembered his last visit there, and the rabble inside who attempted to chase him down after his confrontation with Ocmallum's guards.

As he studied the wall, he tried to assess if he had the strength to throw the head all the way to the inner courtyard. He took a few steps back and imagined it landing in the middle of a group of sleepy-eyed men, struggling to discern if they were having a nightmare or were being invaded.

"Wait," Brunnlyn whispered.

"What is it? Would you like to throw it?" Dulnear asked.

"No," his friend answered. "Look. Do you notice anything strange about the walls?"

Dulnear studied the top of the wall carefully. Sighing, he answered, "There are no guards."

"That is odd," Onclaid added.

"Perhaps it is a shift change," Dulnear surmised.

"Perhaps," Brunnlyn grunted.

"Well, let us not waste this opportunity," Dulnear said. He then took a parchment from his coat pocket. A threatening note was scribbled on it, and he attached it to the head with a stake he had whittled from a tree branch.

"I cannot believe you are handling that thing," Onclaid gagged. "It smells like a ratsnake."

"Smelling many ratsnakes these day?" Dulnear jabbed.

"Just throw it over before the odor is forever embedded in my nostrils," his friend implored.

Dulnear took a few steps back and cocked his arm back as far as it would go. Leading with his hip, he threw the head over the wall and listened for a thud. When he was fairly certain the head landed where he had hoped, he listened for the panicked voices of Ocmallum's men. "Here it comes," he chuckled.

"I do not hear anything," Brunnlyn observed.

"Just wait," Dulnear whispered as he moved closer to the wall and waited for the small army inside to stir. "They are probably still sleeping."

Finally, a voice from inside cried out, "Hey!"

"Looks like you were right," Onclaid noted.

The three men turned away from the castle wall and prepared to run back to their horses. However, Dulnear was perplexed. "It is too quiet. I do not even hear movement."

Brunnlyn squinted and pursed his lip together. Drawing his sword, he croaked, "Wait here."

"I hope he knows what he is doing," Dulnear expressed.

"I am sure he does," Onclaid assured him.

Suddenly, there was a thud at their feet and both men jumped back. "The head!" Dulnear shouted, and he took out his sword. Looking up, he could see Brunnlyn standing over them.

"What news?" Onclaid called up.

"There is no one here!" the man yelled.

"And what of the man who cried out?" Dulnear asked.

"He was the only one. Just a groundskeeper who was up early!" Brunnlyn answered.

An uneasy sensation began to make its way up Dulnear's spine. Swallowing, he asked, "Where is everyone else?"

"I am sorry, my friend," Brunnlyn said. "According to the groundskeeper, Ocmallum and his men left for Laor yesterday."

## CHAPTER TWELVE
# AN UNLIKELY ARMY

Son, Maren, and Aesef rode east toward Gale Hill. The road somehow felt less friendly, and Son wondered how Maren could sleep so soundly leaned against his back. As their journey came nearer to its end, he could feel a nervousness begin to bubble up inside of him. He hoped Henry had fulfilled his promise to train the townspeople to fight, and that the beast Verrox hadn't tried to eat him.

"Are you nervous about returning home?" Aesef asked as if he knew the boy's thoughts.

Son kept his eyes on the road and squinted as he answered, "I suppose I'm afraid I won't have a home to return to."

The old farmer gave a long, understanding, "Mmmm-mm," and moved his horse so it was alongside Son's. "What's important is the family you've formed," he said. "Houses can burn and be rebuilt, farms can be replanted, and possessions can be reacquired. But what you have is special, like none I've ever seen before. Cherish that. Thank the Great Father for that, and look after each other."

The boy was strangely consoled by Aesef's words. He thought about how valiantly his friends had fought for each other, and for him. He was grateful for them, and knew his life had been enriched because of their companionship. "Thank you," he said. "I suppose I'm just fearing the worst."

The man gave an understanding nod. "I suppose we all are," he said. "We will approach the farm stealthily and see what awaits us. Then, you can decide what the next move should be."

"Okay," Son replied. He thought for a moment and added, "Thank you for standing with me. It's an honor to be your friend."

"Likewise," Aesef said. "Likewise."

As the three drew closer to the farm, Son dismounted his horse and led it off the road.

"Where are we going?" Maren asked. She was still sitting atop the horse and looked as if she had just woken up from a deep sleep.

"Aesef and I are going the rest of the way by foot," he answered. "We want to check out Gale Hill to make sure it's safe before we return."

Maren slid off the side of the horse, landing awkwardly on her feet. Smoothing out the front of her dress, she insisted, "I'm going with you."

"Someone needs to stay with the horses," the boy

disagreed. He knew he was only telling a partial truth, and was really just wanting her to stay behind in case she made too much noise when they went to inspect the farm.

"But we can tie them to a tree," she argued.

Son took a long, exasperated breath. He didn't want to waste time fighting with her so he made her promise to be silent until they returned to the horses.

After Aesef had dismounted and a place for the horses was found a short distance from the road, they walked quietly toward the farm. As they did, Son did his best to keep his imagination from getting the best of him. Even though they had only been gone for a short time, it felt like several days, and he worried once again that there would be no home for him to return to.

When the farm was in sight from a distance, they jogged into the trees that lined their path and crept through them as they approached. As they drew closer, the noise of clanging metal could be heard.

"Swords," Maren whispered as she froze in place.

Son stopped moving too, and listened intently. "It sure sounds like it," he agreed. "I hope we're not too late."

"We should get a closer look," Aesef chimed in. "It's always a good idea to confirm with our eyes what we hear with our ears."

"Okay," the boy murmured. He then withdrew his sword and added, "Just in case."

The three made their way through the woods around the property until the ground began to slope downward and most of the farm was visible to them. From their position, they could see a mob of shabby-looking people rhythmically clashing swords as a tall, fur-clad man walked around examining them.

"What's happening?" Son blurted. He couldn't understand what he was seeing, and the strange sight had him anxious for answers.

"There's Henry!" Maren pointed out, and thrust her finger toward the barkeep who was moving in sync with the crowd.

"I don't think they're fighting," Aesef observed. "I believe that tall fellow is training them."

Son looked closer. Upon further investigation, he realized the farmer was right. But he had so many questions about what they were witnessing.

"Well, how do you feel about going home now?" the old man asked.

The question sat strangely with the boy. Not knowing how to answer, he simply said, "Let's go get the horses."

As Son rode down the path toward the house, the crowd looked much larger to him than it did from the woods. He, Maren, and Aesef halted near the front door and tied their horses to a post. As they did, Henry ran to them.

"Welcome back!" he greeted cheerily. "What do you think of all these people?"

Son scratched his head and slowly dragged his eyes over the crowd. "I see most of the town is here," he observed. "But who are the rest of these people? And why do they look like slaves?"

"Because they are," Henry explained. "They just keep coming."

Son felt a strange sensation at hearing the barkeep's words. "W-What do you mean?" he stammered.

"I mean that word has spread about your stand against Ocmallum, and slaves from all over Aun are coming to stand with you," Henry explained.

Dumbfounded, Son just stared at the man until he felt Aesef's hand on his shoulder. "But how?" he muttered. "I mean... "

Henry glanced at the training slaves, then back at the boy. "The slaver king is so hellbent on making an example out of you that he has pulled most of his men away from their camps so they can join him," he began. "Which has left many slaves unguarded or under-guarded."

"So they're breaking out to join us?" Maren jumped in.

"That's exactly what's happening," their friend confirmed. "I've never seen anything like it."

Son stood in stunned silence as he reflected on the news. Finally, he said, "I... uh... didn't mean to start a revolution. Just wanted to do the right thing."

Aesef's hand squeezed the boy's shoulder. He leaned in and spoke into his ear, "I'm honored to stand beside you."

Son could feel Maren's hand squeezing his as she whispered, "Me too."

Son took a deep breath to suppress a tear that was wanting to emerge from his eye. "Well." He swallowed. "Let's make sure everyone has food, water, and weapons. Maren, would you please check on the animals and make sure the kottur hasn't eaten any of them?"

"Uh-huh," she sang, and skipped off to the barn.

"What would you like me to do?" Henry asked.

"You can head back to our trainees," Son said. "I'll be with you in a moment to meet our Saor friend, and introduce myself to our makeshift army."

"Yessir," the barkeep smiled. He returned to the crowd of slaves training on the other side of the garden.

Son took a moment to ponder what was happening all around him. When he left for Blackcloth, he had a terrible but righteous sense that his stand against the slavers was the right thing to do, however futile. Now, he felt a tide of momentum swelling alongside him, and he wasn't sure what to do next.

"Lead them," a voice spoke softly behind him.

The boy was so lost in thought that he had forgotten that Aesef was still with him. Turning back to the old farmer, he asked, "What?"

"Lead them," the man repeated. "No one has ever stood up to the slavers the way you have. You have held Ocmallum at the edge of a sword. You know he is only a man, despite the reputation he has painted for himself. Lead them, inspire them, help them to see with new eyes and set them free in ways they didn't know they could be free."

Son's legs felt like they could barely hold him up. Never had he felt so inadequate for a task. He weighed his response to the man carefully. After searching for words for what felt like forever, he finally said, "Okay. But I can't do it alone. This is a task that is going to take all of us, and I'm going to need the help of my friends."

Aesef smiled, and his eyes seemed to swell as he once

again reached out for Son's shoulder. "And that is why I believe you are right for the job," he said.

The boy inhaled and let out a great sigh. "But I feel so unqualified," he confessed.

"That's okay," the old farmer encouraged. "The Great Father does not always call the qualified. But he does qualify the called."

Son thought about the man's words. "I hope you're right," he muttered. "I hope you're right for all of our sakes."

## CHAPTER THIRTEEN

# GALE HILL

Dulnear, Brunnlyn, and Onclaid rode hard along the westerly road toward Laor. A deep regret was settling into Dulnear's heart as he believed their mission to destroy the borb plantation was futile.

"Ride!" he shouted to his friends, though the three of them were already going as fast as their horses could carry them.

The mid-morning, dull-gray sky sat over the land like an uneasy dream, and it seemed as if the passing fields themselves were fatigued with despair. The man from the north could think of nothing else but Faymia, and how he should have cared more for returning to her side than sending a message to Ocmallum. "Ride!" he called out again.

"We cannot be any more riding!" Brunnlyn called back. "And if our horses collapse under the strain, we will be set back all the more!"

Dulnear kept pace but decided not to drive his animal any harder. Peering down the road, he could see what looked like a swarm of men marching in a haphazard fashion.

"A garrison!" Onclaid announced.

Dulnear couldn't believe their luck. They had nearly overtaken the men who had left the slaver king's estate the morning before. He considered his next move carefully, not wanting to delay his return to Gale Hill any further.

"We should not engage yet," Brunnlyn informed. "We must make our way around them and get to where we'll have the aid of our other Saor brothers."

Dulnear swallowed and slowed his horse. "South of the road would be wisest," he told his friends. "There is not much but field and farm between here and the sea."

The man from the north had a fleeting sense of relief at the prospect of overtaking the garrison. He took a deep breath and resolved to reunite with his wife without hindrance. He sped in a southwesterly arc as his countrymen followed.

While moving swiftly through the countryside, Dulnear's mind displayed pictures of his beloved, their friends, and Gale Hill. He could feel in his stomach the desire to be there again with them. No matter how fast he traveled, it felt as if the ground beneath him was unchanged and he still had a terribly long way to go. Saying a prayer, he coaxed just a little more speed from his horse.

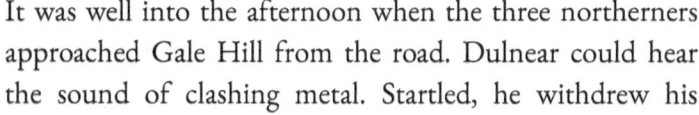

It was well into the afternoon when the three northerners approached Gale Hill from the road. Dulnear could hear the sound of clashing metal. Startled, he withdrew his sword and sped toward the farm. When it was in full view, he gasped at the scene.

"Ah, good. It looks like the other Saor have arrived," Brunnlyn exclaimed. "And it looks like the lad is training the locals how to fight!"

"And slaves, by the look of them," Onclaid added.

Dulnear couldn't believe his eyes. The entire estate had been turned into a training camp. There were rows of makeshift tents toward the edges of the property, and where there once was a large garden, young and old were learning how to fight. Son was teaching them all alongside a handful of left-handed northern warriors. He rode down to greet the boy, but as he did, he noticed the absence of his wife from within the crowd.

"Dulnear!" Son called out. His face lit up at the sight of his friend.

"Son!" the man called back.

At the sound of the lively greeting, many of the would-be combatants lowered their weapons and turned their attention toward the reunited friends. Dulnear dismounted his horse and lifted the boy off the ground with a warm embrace.

"Can you believe what's happening here?" Son beamed. "They've all come to help."

Dulnear was still in awe of the developments around him. He looked his friend in the eyes and spoke. "I am incredibly proud of you. I knew you had it within you to lead."

The boy wrapped his arms around the neck of his mentor. "Thank you," he said. "I'm only passing on what you have taught me."

Dulnear could feel the presence of his two northern companions standing behind him. "You know Brunnlyn," he began. "And this is another friend, and Saor brother, Onclaid."

"Pleased to meet you," Onclaid bowed. He then stepped toward the boy, extended his left hand and added, "I have heard much about you."

"Thank you, and it's a pleasure to meet you," Son smiled as he gave the man the heartiest of left-handed hand-shakes. "And it's great to see you as well, Brunnlyn," he added. "Thank you for keeping my friend safe."

"You have no idea what an arduous task that is," the man replied with a nearly imperceptible wink.

Dulnear moved his eyes to the ground for moment, then back toward the boy. He wanted to continue his greetings, and he had many questions, but there was one thing he wanted to know above all else. "Son, can we talk in private?" he asked.

"Sure," the boy answered. "There are people in the house preparing food. Let's walk to the barn."

The two walked over to the barn as Brunnlyn and Onclaid joined with the other Saor brothers and resumed the training that was taking place before they arrived.

When Dulnear stepped into the barn, he was greeted by more surprises. Toward the back of the barn, he saw Maren sleeping soundly, draped across the back of the great beast Verrox. Next to them was Earl the mule, who was also snoozing away. "What is happening here?" he muttered.

"Oh, Maren doesn't like the constant coming and going happening in the house so she comes out here for peace and quiet," Son explained.

"I understand that, but what is she doing atop the kottur?"

"Oh, they've become great friends. She even lets Maren ride her," the boy explained. "But I think Earl has become quite jealous. He just follows them around and mopes. Every once in a while he'll nudge her to see if she wants to get on."

"Well, now I have seen everything," Dulnear grinned. "A kottur that will be ridden, and an insecure donkey."

"It is quite a sight," Son said with a chuckle.

"I am surprised none of this makeshift army has moved into the barn," the man from the north mused.

"That's because Maren is the only one willing to share space with Verrox," Son explained. "Even the other northerners keep away from her."

"Well then... " Dulnear began to say. He was happy to catch up with his friend but there was something weighing heavily on his mind. He peered into the distance for a moment, then asked, "Has Faymia made it back? I do long to see her."

"Not yet," the boy said. "But I'm sure she'll be back very soon."

The northern warrior recalled the garrison along the road toward Laor. He found it difficult to suppress imaginations of his wife being captured, or worse. "Perhaps I should ride out to make sure she is safe," he thought out loud.

Son's face changed from one of cheer, to one of distress. He reached forward and placed his hand on his mentor's arm. "But that could keep you away for a long time," he fretted. "We don't know when the slavers will be here to attack."

Dulnear took a deep, thoughtful breath. He was torn between retrieving Faymia and staying at Gale Hill. He attempted to say something convincing, but could only utter, "She needs me."

Son seemed to stand a little taller as he spoke. With his hand firmly on the northerner's arm, he answered, "She is not nearly as vulnerable as you imagine her to be. And if you go to find her now, you leave us all the more to be prey to the vilest men in Aun. Faymia would want you to stay."

Dulnear was momentarily taken aback by the confidence of the boy's statement. He considered his words and knew them to be true, even though he didn't want them to be. Locking eyes with him, he said, "You are right. And I have to tell you something. Ocmallum and his men are already approaching Laor. You need to move these people from training to preparation. The battle will be upon us soon."

Son ran out of the barn without a word and began to look for Henry. His heart was racing as the words of his friend sank in. "Henry!" he called out.

Onclaid caught the boy's eye and pointed toward the barkeep who was engaged in a sparring match with one of the other locals. He ran over to him and watched until he felt it an appropriate time to interrupt.

"Henry," he chimed. "We need to speak right away."

The man jogged over to him, out of breath. "What can I do for you?" he asked.

"Training time is over," Son announced. "It's time to prepare for battle."

"What?!" the man choked. "Now?"

"Yes, Ocmallum and his men are nearly here. Give the orders to our northern friends. We must get ready."

Henry swallowed hard and looked around the farm. "How much time do we have?" he asked.

"I want to be ready by sundown," Son instructed. "If we even have that much time."

"I understand," Henry said. "I'll get the northerners to begin digging the trench, and have the rest move their tents to the back of the perimeter."

"Thank you," Son said with a nod. He then ran over to Brunnlyn and Onclaid, who were visiting with one of the other Saor.

"Son," Brunnlyn said. "You look anxious."

"It's time," the boy reported.

"Yes," the northerner answered. "We saw the garrison not far from the village. We were just sharing the news with our friend Dulcara."

Son knew the man he was speaking with. He was an unusual sight for a northerner, with tan skin and ginger hair. He possessed a stern countenance that seemed to fit in poorly with the other Saor, but Son felt at peace with him all the same. "Dulcara, do you remember our preparation plan for Ocmallum's arrival?"

"I do, boy," the man replied with a gravely voice. He then turned and signaled to the other northern warriors who had been training the would-be army. Some of them were already in motion thanks to Henry's help, and those who were not began to give instruction to the groups they were leading.

Suddenly, it seemed as if everyone on the estate was moving frantically. Tents were being taken down and moved, men were digging along the boundaries of the property, and Maren came riding out of the barn atop the fierce Verrox.

"Son!" Maren called out. "I saw Dulnear!" She was sitting atop Verrox, holding onto the scruff of her neck.

"I know. You were sleeping in the barn when he returned," Son replied. "Did he tell you that the slavers are almost here?"

"Uh-huh," she said with excitement building in her voice.

As she came closer, the kottur dragged its enormous tongue across the boy's face. He tried to hide his disgust so as not to offend the beast. Scratching at its whiskers, he asked, "Are you ready for battle, Verrox?"

"She is," Maren answered for the animal.

"Well then, I've fashioned some armor for her," Son began. "If you look near my workbench in the barn, you'll see a mail blanket and some pieces to protect her legs."

"Really?!" the girl chirped.

"Really," he replied. "Go and get her ready, then bring Earl out to the northerners. Maybe he can help them dig the trench."

"Okay!" Maren said with an awkward salute. She then

tugged at the fur behind the kottur's ears and it trotted back to the barn.

As time rapidly ticked on, it seemed as if the farm grew more alive. Slaves and townspeople relocated tents, armed themselves, and applied makeshift breastplates and helmets. The seven Saor brethren continued to dig a ditch around the property, and a handful of people, led by Aesef, came pouring out of the house carrying platters of roast pheasant and potatoes.

At the sight of the old farmer and the plates of food, a few of the scurrying people jogged over to the side of the barn and returned to the front of the house with long tables for the food to be set upon.

"Aesef, did you hear?" Son called out as the man directed his companions to lay out the meal.

"Did I hear that the slavers are on the way?" the farmer said. "I think we've all heard." He then walked over to the boy and asked, "Have all of the preparations been made?"

"I think so," Son replied. "I just hope it's enough."

"I do too," Aesef breathed.

Son looked around the farm at all the activity. He felt woefully inadequate to take on Ocmallum and his army. He was grateful for all of the neighbors and friends that had come to help, even though many of them had never held swords before. It suddenly occurred to him. "Phel and the other farmhands have not yet arrived. Do you think they'll make it on time?" he asked Aesef.

The old farmer looked out toward the road, then back at his young friend. "He'll be here," he said confidently. "And if I know his reputation with the other workers, they'll be here too."

Son felt his shoulders relax a bit at Aesef's confidence. He watched the tribe of escaped slaves, well-meaning townspeople, and one-handed northerners make their way toward the tables of food, and was deeply moved that they would make his cause their own. "You better eat something," he told his friend. "It's going to be a long night."

---

Before Son knew it, every hand on Gale Hill was standing near the front of the house. He made sure everyone had enough to eat before turning to the table to feed himself. To his disappointment, all had been eaten, and his stomach growled to inform him that such was often the result of leadership. He sighed and looked around. It was a strange group to him, but he was encouraged to see such lively conversation between them all, especially between slaves and northerners.

"Here you go, lad," a friendly voice spoke from behind him.

When Son turned around, he saw Aesef standing there with a plate full of food. Not only was he tickled that he was the only one with the distinction of having a plate, but a sense of relief that he wouldn't be fighting on an empty stomach came over him too. "Thank you!" the boy beamed.

"I couldn't let you go hungry," the old farmer said with a kind smile.

As Son eagerly consumed every morsel on his plate, he could feel his strength grow and, for a mere fleeting moment, he felt like he and his band of fighters could take on Ocmallum's army.

When he was finished, he turned toward Aesef to thank him again. The man cheerfully took the boy's plate and gestured toward the crowd.

When Son turned back toward everyone, he was taken aback as he saw that they had all grown quiet and were turned toward him. "What's going on?" the boy whispered to his friend.

"I think they're expecting you to say something," his friend whispered back.

His heart raced and his palms began to sweat. He had fought against northern warriors, slavers, and Ocmallum himself, but the thought of speaking to a listening crowd intimidated him like nothing before. As he searched his mind for something to say, he could see Dulnear standing toward the front of the crowd, and recalled how the man gave up his inheritance to purchase Faymia's freedom. He saw Brunnlyn, who took the wrath of Dulnear's enemies upon himself. He saw Henry, who was willing to confront the slavers even though he had never held a sword. And he saw his dear Maren, who was becoming a wise young woman even after great loss and the presence of the graymind.

Clearing his throat, he breathed, "Thank you. Many, if not all of you, have chosen to fight alongside myself and my friends when looking away would be an easier, safer course of action."

"Perhaps we lack sense," Henry joked.

"Perhaps," Son chuckled, relaxing a bit. "But those who dare greatly are often called crazy. And every victory is considered mad until after it's been accomplished. I don't see crazy standing here with me today. I see slaves who have aspired to take up a cause greater than they've known before. I see northerners who have broken away from petty feuds to use their swords to fight for peace. I see my neighbors drawing a line in the sand to proclaim that the enemy is not welcome at their doorstep. And I see my family... "

The boy took a deep breath. Doing his best to hold back a tear, he continued. "I see my family, who would rather fight and die beside me than to live without me, and I, them."

He glanced at Dulnear, who was wiping a tear from his eye, then at Maren, who was doing the same. "Today marks the beginning of a new era in Aun," he continued. "An era where bullies, slavers, and ne'er-do-wells no longer get to dictate or manipulate our lives with fear and intimidation. Win, lose, or draw, they will think twice before rolling into one of our villages to trap our people or entice our children. The scars they accumulate today will forever be a reminder that we will choose the difficult path. We will fight for our villages, and we will not allow them to do as they please without consequence!"

Son could hear his own voice echo into the gray afternoon sky as he finished his speech. He swallowed and looked around at the silent faces staring back at him. He was convinced that they all thought he was mad. Then Maren began to whisper, "For Aun, for Aun, for Aun, for Aun."

Dulnear heard the girl and began to follow, "For Aun, for Aun, for Aun."

Others in the crowd joined in, getting louder, until Son found himself shouting in unison with them, "For Aun! For Aun! For Aun! For Aun!"

The chorus grew louder until it sounded as if thousands of voices were ringing out with a battle cry. Son didn't want it to end. He poured all of his attention onto this moment in an effort to will time to stand still. In this singular instant, he could feel the nearness of the Great Father, and a sense that all was not hopeless.

"That was a fine speech, boy," Dulnear said as he placed his hand on Son's shoulder.

"Thank you," Son smiled, though it somehow felt awkward to receive a compliment in the given situation.

The two found themselves walking into the barn together. As the afternoon light was fading, Son lit lanterns throughout. He made his way over to his workbench, which was cluttered with odd shapes of iron and leather.

"You have come a long way," the man from the north added. "In fact, I have taught you all that I know."

Son was taken aback by the man's words. He thought about the first time he had asked Dulnear to teach him how to fight, and how strange the lessons seemed to him at the time. Despite what his mentor had just said, he could hardly believe he was a match for him, even with the use of both hands. "You mean I have nothing left to learn?" he asked.

"I did not say that," Dulnear chuckled. "Your hand is growing mighty. But the heart of the warrior and the hand of the warrior are two very different things. They both need to grow, for without the heart, the hand can be dangerous. And without the hand, the heart can be vulnerable."

Son knew well the heart of the man who spoke to him. He knew that his heart was good. He had watched him stay his hand on many occasions, and often marveled at the gentleness of such a strong man. He had a yearning to be like his friend. "How do I grow my heart?" he asked.

"First, I must say that you already have the bravest, kindest heart I have ever known in a lad," the man began. "So when I say that a warrior must grow their heart, I do not mean to imply that you have a bad one. But, just as skills in swordsmanship must continually be developed, growing the heart is a lifelong pursuit. It is often developed through the way we walk through difficulty. It is also grown by deliberate acts of sacrificial love and kindness."

Son remembered the many kind things Dulnear had done for him, and for Faymia, and Maren, often without thanks or reciprocation.

"You're pretty good at that," Son complimented.

Dulnear looked at the ground and scratched the top of his head. Pursing his lips, he breathed, "If you only knew, Son. I still have such a long way to go. There is still much violence and anger in me. Even while out on my mission, I made regrettable decisions."

The boy shuddered to think what decisions his friend had made, and chose not to ask. "What else can be done?" he asked.

The man from the north took a deep breath and exhaled as his eyes peered off into the distance. "The Great Father," he said.

Son remembered his encounter with the Great Father. It was one that stayed strangely fresh in his mind. He tried to speak the question that was on his heart, but could only mutter, "How?"

Dulnear took another deep breath and answered, "Trust. Something wonderful happens when we realize that the Great Father cares for us even more than we do, and that his wisdom is greater than our wisdom." He then scratched his cheek and continued. "When we lay down our petty pride, of which I have much, and trust him, and let him direct our paths, our hearts grow."

Son thought about the impending battle approaching Gale Hill and wondered if he had followed the Great Father or his own desire to take a stand. "Will he help us defeat the slavers?" he asked.

"I do not know, but I am trusting him," the man from the north answered.

The boy was unsatisfied by his friend's answer. "But will we win?" he asked again.

"I do not know," Dulnear repeated. He then peered into Son's eyes, and spoke more slowly. "Real trust is larger than success or failure. It means that whether we are victorious, or face total defeat, I know that the Great Father is for me."

Son again recalled his moment with the Great Father. How it came on the heels of nearly dying in battle. But he still found it difficult to accept what his friend was saying. "It's just that," he began, when an unexpected catch appeared in his throat. He pushed back the reflex to tear up and continued. "It's just that I don't want anyone to die."

Dulnear whispered a small chuckle, and said with a sad smile, "Live, die, it matters not. For you never know how the tales of your bravery will inspire others. And the small ripple you make may very well grow into waves that wash away evil. Besides, this life is but a breath. Eternity awaits us in the hill country of Neahemel, where death and sorrow will be no more."

Son held onto that thought, and remembered his brief visit to Neahemel. He also did his best to lay everyone and everything into the hands of the Great Father. As he did, his thoughts were interrupted by his friend.

"What is this?" the northerner asked. He was pointing to a strange tangle of iron and leather on the workbench.

"Oh, that's for you!" Son announced. "Instead of an iron fist, or a knife-hand, it's a hand that actually holds a sword."

Dulnear's eyes grew wide as he picked the strange apparatus up from the table. "This is amazing," he pronounced. "Can I put it on?"

"Of course," Son chirped. "I'll help you."

The boy loosened the leather belt that connected to the forearm sheath and iron fist. The fist resembled a cannon-ball with a hole in its center. It sat partially inside a metal cup that had a large clasp attached to it. He then tightened the belt, pulling on it until he could barely buckle it in place.

"You have outdone yourself," the man from the north said as he marveled at the strange gadget attached to his arm. He then withdrew his sword with his left hand and asked, "How does it work?"

"Just slide the hilt into the hole," Son answered. "Then swing the clasp up and fasten it."

Dulnear did as he was instructed. There was a satisfying clicking sound as the clasp was set in place. He turned away from the table and held out his sword. As he did, he noticed that there was a small amount of play between the fist and the cup-socket it rested in. "It even moves similar to a wrist!" he shouted. He then grasped the hilt with his left hand beneath the metal hand and lunged forward. "Son, how can I thank you?" he asked.

"You already have," Son smiled. "But perhaps you should get a little practice in before stepping out to show your friends."

"Very good idea," the northerner replied as he swung his sword in an awkward figure-of-eight in front of him.

Son was filled with joy that his friend was pleased with his gift. He watched him for a bit longer before leaving the barn to check on the preparations for battle. As he walked out into the early evening air, he was surprised by how quickly the night had come, and how quiet the farm had grown. He slowly moved his eyes across Gale Hill, making sure everything was in its place. As he did, he noticed the silhouette of three figures peering in from the road.

## CHAPTER FOURTEEN

# FIRST BLOOD

"Dulnear," Son whispered. His friend was still standing behind him, acclimating himself to the new hand the boy had made him.

"Hmm?" the northerner muttered, still focused on maneuvering his sword with his right hand once again.

"Dulnear," Son repeated. "Someone is spying on us."

The man from the north released the clasp at the bottom of his new iron fist, took the sword from it, and sheathed it. "I'll have to realign my scabbard," he whispered as he tiptoed over to his friend.

"See?" Son breathed. "Three figures near the road." The hairs on his neck stood up as he wondered if this was the beginning of the battle.

Dulnear squinted into the darkness. He then looked out toward the western edge of the farm where his northern friends had just finished filling the trench they had dug with oil. "Come with me," he said, and began to jog toward them.

Son ran behind his friend, wondering what the man

had in mind. When they reached the Saor brothers, he noticed that they had all been watching the three figures.

"Kerraic," Dulnear said quietly to the other northerners.

"Kerraic," Brunnlyn grunted. It was a common, casual greeting that was often heard among men from Tuas-arum.

"It looks like we have three onlookers," Dulnear announced.

"Yes, we have been observing them since dusk," Onclaid chimed in. "Should we kill them?"

"No," Son interrupted. His heart suddenly pulsed in his chest. Such a question had never been posed to him, and it felt wrong and strange.

"Perhaps detain them," Dulnear suggested.

Son thought for a moment as he stared at the three motionless figures. "Brunnlyn," he said. "Can you light an arrow and send it over their heads?"

"Of course," the northerner replied. He wrapped a strip of cloth around an arrow, dipped it in a nearly empty jug of oil, and lit it from a nearby torch. He then sent it flying through the air above the three watchers.

The arrow sailed above the road, illuminating the figures. As it did, one of them could be seen drawing back a bow. Just before the light of the overhead flame disappeared, Son noticed it was a woman wearing an eyepatch. "It's Faymia!" he alerted the northerners.

"Faymia!" Dulnear cried out. "It is she, and two friends from the Ohdium!"

"Let them through!" Son yelled, though no one in particular was keeping them at a distance.

Son and Dulnear ran toward the road just as Faymia

was running toward them. They met near the northeast corner of the house and the man from the north lifted his wife off the ground and squeezed her so tightly that Son worried for her safety.

"You made it back!" Dulnear sang.

"Did you think I wouldn't?" Faymia asked.

The northerner lowered his wife to the ground and admitted, "Well, I was a bit worried."

Faymia adjusted her eyepatch, which had slid out of place by her husband's embrace, and smiled. "Have faith, my husband," she said. "I couldn't leave you here to fight the slavers by yourself."

"We're not by ourselves," Son broke in. "Look at all the people who came to help us."

Faymia turned toward the boy and smiled proudly. "And you, lad. You did all this?" She then hugged his neck and added, "It's good to see you again."

"Most of them were here when Maren and I returned from Blackcloth," Son explained. "Some of them are escaped slaves who came to fight for their freedom."

Just then, Jarmour and Argach came jogging up to meet them. "Thank you for not killing us with your flaming arrow," Argach said with a wry smile.

Son chuckled and answered, "We thought you might be spies."

"When we arrived and saw all of the people, we were afraid Gale Hill had already been besieged," Faymia explained.

"I saw many of Ocmallum's men on the road," Dulnear said. "Even with all of these people, we are still woefully outnumbered. Is two fighters all that the Ohdium could spare?"

"More will come," Jarmour stated.

Son heard the man's words but was comforted very little by them. "Our enemy is nearly upon us. Are you sure your fighters will be here?"

Jarmour looked as if he were trying diligently to not look offended. "Le'as is a man of his word," he exclaimed. "He will show."

"As will Thuaid," Argach added. "And you have my sword until he does."

The boy felt a bit embarrassed for openly questioning the good will of Faymia's companions. "I trust you," he muttered. "Please, let's get you three something to eat, and some rest. It's going to be a long night."

Maren nestled closely on one side of Faymia while Dulnear sat next to her on the other side. Also seated at the table were Son, Jarmour, and Argach. There was a strange tension in the kitchen as the three new arrivals ate what could be found in the cupboards. When they had eaten their fill, Son jumped up and began to clear their plates from the table.

"So," Jarmour broke the silence. "Have you no lookouts?"

"What do you mean?" Son asked.

"I mean that we stood by the road for quite a while before anyone took action. It would be good to know that the slavers aren't able to simply take a position at the edge of the road as they please," the man explained.

Son felt a bit embarrassed. "Our northern friends had you in their sights the moment you came upon Gale Hill," he explained.

"What about scouts?" Jarmour pressed. "You are asking the Ohdium to risk its fighters but we are all prone to a surprise attack."

The boy fought back the urge to defend his leadership. He knew the man was right, but the conversation made him feel exposed. Clearing his throat, he replied, "You make a very good point." He then turned toward Dulnear and asked, "Do you think one of the brethren would accompany one of our friends from Laor to scout the eastern road?"

The man from the north nodded, whispered something to his love, and excused himself.

As Dulnear stepped out of the house, Son studied the uncertain faces that sat before him. "I'm going to check on our preparations," he announced. "We still have poles to sharpen, slaves to arm, and a trebuchet to complete."

"A trebuchet?" Maren perked up.

"That's right," Son confirmed. "If we have time," he added. Turning his attention toward Faymia, he said, "Once the three of you are rested, please see Henry. He will fill you in on our plans for Ocmallum's arrival."

---

It was late into the night, and Son watched Maren sleep as she lay on the barn floor and rested her back against the lightly snoring Verrox. Earl lay next to them, kicking his feet occasionally as he dreamed whatever dreams mules dream on tense, late-autumn nights.

The boy then turned his attention toward Dulnear, who was standing at the workbench while Faymia helped him make some final adjustments to the fighting hand he had fashioned for him.

None of them spoke, and the barely audible flickering of the torches was the only thing that could be heard. The sound fascinated Son because it could be heard over the throbbing in his ears, and he reckoned the throbbing to be the loudest noise in the world.

He sat on a wooden chair he had made a while back. He had made several iterations of the chair and they were scattered about the barn. He was positioned so he could see out of the barn, and had left the door open just enough to get a view of the road, even though he could only see a handful of torch-bearing slaves and townsfolk walking about.

Son watched his friends and took a deep breath, as if trying to drink in the moment. In his mind, he prayed earnestly that this would not be their last time together. Like a blow to the back of his head, it struck him how he had failed to truly enjoy the moments they participated in together and be grateful of the life they had lived. "More time," he whispered. "Just a little more."

From the road came the sound of a horse whinny. It jarred the boy upright, and he stood to get a better look into the darkness.

"Scout!" a voice called out, and the animal trotted all the way to the barn before coming to a full stop.

Son recognized the shape of the man on the horse. He

called back to his friends. "It's Gastoeg," he announced. "The Saor who went out to scout."

Dulnear and Faymia joined Son at the door and they jogged out to see what the man had to report.

"Wait!" Dulnear ordered. He held out his arm to keep his wife and friend from going further.

Just then, the body of the northern scout slumped over dead before sliding to the ground with a thud.

---

Faymia embraced her husband, longing to never let go of him. Now that it was time to execute their battle plan, she didn't want to. "Is it really time?" she asked.

"I am afraid that it is," Dulnear said as he held her tight. "We will give Gastoeg a proper burial when the battle is over."

"I was hoping we'd have more time," she lamented.

"As was I," he whispered.

Faymia drew a deep breath and mustered a brave face as she slowly broke their embrace. "Promise me something," she said as she gazed into Dulnear's eyes.

"Anything."

"Promise me that you will mind yourself out there."

"Of course," he said. However, his face betrayed that he didn't fully understand what he was promising.

"Don't be impulsive," she continued. "Don't fight out of anger. Use your skill. Return to me when this is over."

The man from the north nodded his head in agreement and added, "If you promise to do the same."

"Then I'll see you soon," Faymia smiled, and she ran off toward the road.

As she jogged through the rows of townspeople and runaway slaves, she could see Argach and Jarmour standing with a group of northerners at the trench that sat nearest the road. Beyond the trench was a makeshift platform that was nearly as tall as the house, fortified with oddly shaped scraps of wood and iron.

"So, that's our home for the night?" Faymia asked, gesturing toward the tower.

"Indeed it is," Argach answered.

"This is insane," the woman replied.

Argach smiled. "Insanity seems to be normal for you and your friends. But your insanity is what united the Rift," he said.

"We should go," Jarmour interrupted.

Faymia looked over at a nearby northerner who was holding a torch. She gave him a knowing nod, and he did the same in return.

Along with Argach and Jarmour, she hopped over the trench and made her way to the elevated platform. As they approached, there was a whooshing sound that echoed into the night. She turned around and saw the wall of fire where there once was a trench filled with oil.

Faymia's heart raced, and her hands shook at the thought of the three of them being cut off from the rest of the farm. She ascended the questionable wooden steps to the top of the watchtower, followed by her companions. "The northerners assembled this so quickly," she observed. "I hope it holds for the night."

"Hopefully, we won't need it to," Argach assured, and he took his bow in hand.

Faymia and Jarmour also drew their bows. They each turned to see down the road. Facing east, they waited.

⊶────────

It was the time of morning that still felt like night. In the faint, hazy, charcoal light, Faymia, through tired eyes, gazed down the road and could see black silhouettes of men on horseback in the distance. They moved slowly and confidently as rows of marching fighters came up behind them.

"They're approaching," the woman whispered.

"I see that," Argach whispered in return. "Say the word, and we will release our arrows."

Jarmour readied an arrow. "I'm ready when you are," he stated.

"Just a little closer," Faymia instructed. "We don't want them retreating to the fields."

The woman's hands began to sweat and she took deep breaths through her nose to calm herself. With each step the slavers took, it seemed as if their footsteps grew louder, pounding in sync with the pulsating she felt in her ears. Her shoulder began to ache as she waited, but she was afraid to release the tension on her bow for fear that she wouldn't be able to prepare her arrow again in time. Trying desperately not to shake from the pain, she watched the enemy until they were a stone's throw from the platform.

Finally, they were within reach and well illuminated by the fire that burned behind the tower.

"Now!" Faymia called to her companions, and they began releasing arrows into the marching horde.

Immediately, the three took down the horsemen that led the brigade. The fighters that followed drew their swords.

"It looks like they have no archers," Jarmour observed as he planted another arrow into a confused mercenary.

"At least not within this group," Faymia replied.

Several of the slaver fighters began to move toward the tower. As they did, Argach took aim and quickly did away with them with his bow.

"They may have underestimated us," Jarmour grinned as he continued to fire into the crowd. "I think they were only expecting the boy and his friends."

As the slaver mercenaries continued to crowd around the platform, Faymia could see the number of their enemies more clearly. She glanced down the road once more and her heart nearly beat from her chest. "There's no end to them!" she announced.

From the platform where she stood, out into the hazy, dark horizon, the road was covered with the filth of hired men willing to strike down a boy for a few coins.

"Fight on!" Jarmour encouraged. "We don't have the luxury of hand-wringing."

Faymia knew he was speaking the truth. The crowd around the platform grew thicker, and she continued to fire arrows into it.

"We're halfway out!" Argach called out from the other side of the platform. "These animals keep coming!"

Faymia fired an arrow into the neck of a climbing fighter. She then looked over to see their supply of arrows dwindling at the center of the platform. Before reaching for another, she felt at her waist to be sure her sword was still in its place.

As the circle of slaver soldiers grew around them, she hoped and prayed that she would live to see her husband again. The three fought on until the last arrow. Faymia then withdrew her sword and began hacking at the men as they tried to reach them.

Argach and Jarmour were also out of ammunition, and swung with their swords at the rabble climbing the makeshift tower.

Finally, one of the slavers climbed over the barricade that surrounded the platform and Faymia quickly removed his right arm before kicking him over the edge. She took the weapon from the dismembered arm he left behind and began to fight with two swords.

"Remind me to never make you angry!" Argach called out as he continued to fight back the mob.

Soon, another goon breached the barricade, and then another. Faymia was growing tired, but knew she must fight on. Finally, she yelled, "Anois!"

At her call, a large iron sheet was dropped across a portion of the wall of fire raging to the south of them. The Saor brethren who lit the flame earlier now ran over the bridge they had created and attacked the slavers with skill and precision.

"Do you think it will work?" Argach asked as he continued to hold the platform.

"It better!" Faymia answered as she chopped at the men climbing toward them.

"I think it is! Look!" Jarmour called out.

Faymia noticed that the attacking rabble was now turning their attention toward the four northerners. Even with their overwhelming numbers, the massive warriors laid them out like rag dolls.

Suddenly, a rock flew through the air, soundly striking one of the Saor brethren in the temple. He stumbled backward, nearly falling into the fire.

"Sling!" Jarmour shouted, and pointed into the crowd where a darkly dressed mercenary was loading another rock into a leather pouch with a strap attached to it.

Just as he began to spin the sling over his head, Faymia spied an arrow that had been kicked against the barricade where she was standing. She quickly armed her bow and launched the arrow into the man's ribcage.

"We need to move onto the next phase," the woman announced. "Let's set this thing ablaze."

Argach retrieved a jug of oil from behind him and began to pour it out onto the platform's floor, keeping it only on the western half.

"Don't get any on you," Jarmour warned as he carefully observed the flow of thugs around them. He then withdrew a fire steel from his pocket and kept an eye on Faymia for her signal.

The woman carefully watched the crowd press in on the northerners. Finally, she signaled to one of them and he began to move backward into the ring of fire as he continued fighting. As he did, the slaver mercenaries followed over the narrow pathway through the flames.

"It's working!" she chirped. "They're creating a gauntlet for these miscreants to pass through if they want to get to their prey."

"Now's the time!" Jarmour interrupted. He nodded toward the break in the flow of fighters. He then struck the oval-shaped piece of steel against the platform, causing a spark to leap from the device.

Immediately, the floor where they were standing burst into flames and the three of them leaped to the ground below. Before they were noticed, they began to run south around the flame wall toward the edge of the farm.

Dulnear, Brunnlyn, and Onclaid stood a distance off, toward the rear of the ring of fire. Behind them stood Son and Maren.

"The enemy has entered the circle," Dulnear announced. He watched as the handful of Saor brethren struck down the rabble as they came through the narrow opening that was created by the metal slab.

Any intruders making it past the Saor northerners were defeated by the townsfolk and runaway slaves led by Henry. During a brief respite, the barkeep glanced back at Dulnear and held up his thumb to let him know the plan was running smoothly. The man from the north returned the gesture, but his mood was not quite so optimistic.

"Where are they?" he wondered out loud.

"They'll be here," Brunnlyn replied.

"I'm sure they cleared the platform," Onclaid also assured.

"This all just seems... " Dulnear began before trailing off.

"Too easy?" Brunnlyn asked, finishing his sentence.

"That's easy for you to say!" a voice yelled from behind the wall of fire blazing behind them.

"It's Faymia!" Maren shouted.

"Quick! Slide that metal over the fire!" Dulnear barked.

Son began to tip a sheet of metal over the flaming trench that separated them from Faymia and her companions from the Ohdium Rift. Dropping it over the flames, he beamed. "You made it!"

Dulnear ran to his love and embraced her. "What did you see?" he asked.

"I saw that it's going to be a long day," she sighed. "There are fighters crowding the road for as far as I could see."

"But, it was still pretty dark," Jarmour interrupted. "Your eyes can play tricks in the dim light."

"Even so," Faymia continued. "This flaming wall better hold, or we're going to need a miracle."

The man from the north squeezed his wife once more. He had seen many battles in his lifetime and wished he could simply take his skill and experience and bestow it upon her. "We will fight on until every one of their resources have been drained and we are standing victorious," he told her.

"If our resources aren't drained first," the woman replied.

The man from the north knew that was a possibility, but wanted to instill hope, even though it felt elusive to him. "We have enough to fulfill our purpose," he assured her. "We have enough."

Son pulled the metal bridge away from the flaming trench and moved closer to Faymia and Dulnear. Rubbing his gloved hands together to shake off the dirt, he added, "We have enough oil to keep the fire burning until tonight, if we need to. And it seems to be doing exactly as we intended."

"And our neighbors are using their newly acquired skills adequately," Dulnear added. "In fact, we may want to strip this dead rabble of anything we can use before tossing their carcasses over the flaming barrier."

"Great idea," Son agreed. "Onclaid, would you mind?"

Onclaid tilted his head and furrowed his brow. "Sure, I am a warrior of noble blood, but I will pick the pockets of corpses for you," he said sarcastically, then jogged off to do what he was asked to do.

Dulnear chuckled. "It looks like you have received your first leadership criticism," he said.

Son shrugged his shoulders. "Is that what that was?"

"We northerners are horrible with sarcasm. The fact that Onclaid even attempted it meant that he was not happy," he explained.

The boy's shoulders drooped down. "Should I send someone else?" he asked.

"I would not," Dulnear replied. "You must understand that in leadership, you will seldom make everyone happy. The quicker you grow accustomed to being unliked, the better."

"Okay," Son said slowly as he grimaced toward no one in particular.

"Now, let us stay the course," the man from the north encouraged. "It will be fully light soon."

Just then, Aesef came running toward them with Phel two steps behind.

"Phel!" Son shouted. "You made it! But what about the others?"

"They will be here," Phel assured.

"Excuse me!" Aesef interrupted. "But the house is on fire!"

Son froze in place as he watched the thatched roof of his house burn. His heart felt sickened as he realized there was no time to rescue any of his belongings that were still inside.

"Archers!" Dulnear yelled.

Son noticed for the first time that there were flaming arrows raining down upon the house from the other side of the burning barrier they had created. Shaking himself from his rumination, he announced, "They're attacking from the west!"

With fighters still streaming in from the north, and archers now firing from the west, the boy hoped the barrier they created for protection wasn't becoming a snare for them to be trapped within.

"With me!" Faymia shouted, and she ran closer to the house, followed by Argach and Jarmour. In the dark-gray early morning sky, they observed the trajectory of the oncoming arrows, then began firing their own arrows in return to hit their assailants.

As Son watched, he realized that their quivers were nearly empty, so he sprinted to the barn to retrieve more arrows for them. Once inside, he began loading his arms with as many as he could carry. Before exiting, he noticed Earl and Verrox sleeping peacefully. "How can you sleep at a time like this?" he yelled with no expectation of an answer from either of them.

Just then, two flaming arrows pierced the roof of the barn.

"No!" the boy shouted as he headed for the door.

Running toward Faymia and her friends from the Ohdium, Son nearly ran over Maren as she seemed to appear in his path out of nowhere. "Get the animals out of the barn!" he shouted as he ran.

Dropping the arrows at the feet of his friends, he watched as they continued to launch them into the early morning sky. Occasionally, he heard the cry of one of the slaver archers, but the hail of flaming arrows did not seem to diminish. Glancing toward the barn, he could see Maren riding out on Verrox, with Earl close behind. He could also see Dulnear, Brunnlyn, and Aesef coming out with armloads of weapons that he had forged, including the remaining arrows.

"This is useless!" Jarmour shouted as he fired another arrow over the house. "We don't even know where they are. Only that they are on the other side of the flaming wall."

Just then, a flaming arrow landed by their feet, setting the grass around it on fire. Son watched as Faymia pulled the arrow from the ground and shot it back through the air. Stomping out the fire, he feared that he and all his friends would burn to death. "This isn't working!" he shouted.

"What would you have us do?" Argach asked as he released the string of his bow.

"I don't know, but we are wasting ammunition," the boy huffed.

Just then, another flaming arrow landed nearby, and another.

"They're going to burn us alive!" he shouted as he attempted to stomp out the burning grass.

"Perhaps I can help!" a voice called from behind the boy.

Phel ran up with a bow in hand and joined the others in firing arrows toward the enemy. Son observed as the man watched the flaming arrows fly into the air, and do his best to land his in the location of the attacking enemy. However, even with an additional archer, the flaming attack did not seem to let up.

Son's heart began to weaken as the fire continued to spread, and the attacks from both directions refused to abate. He took a step back and watched the fiery arrows rain down upon Gale Hill. "Please," he whispered as he returned to stomping out fires and supplying his friends with arrows.

CHAPTER FIFTEEN

# ULTIMATUMS

Furiously sprinting back and forth, Son did his best to keep arrows coming to Faymia, Argach, Phel, and Jarmour. During one of his jogs out to retrieve an arrow, Dulnear stopped him and asked, "What are you doing, boy?"

Son was taken aback by the question, and stood and stared at his friend. "I'm fetching arrows," he answered matter-of-factly.

"The enemy continues to pour in through the north, fiery arrows are raining down from the west, and you are fetching arrows," the man from the north exclaimed. "This is a time to lead. This is your job. Not fetching arrows. Assign one of the dozens of other people here to fetch arrows. You lead."

Son was mildly offended by his friend's words. The situation was dire, and he was doing what he believed to be the best. "In case you haven't noticed, this is rather urgent," he retorted.

"Indeed it is," Dulnear agreed. "But not necessarily the

most important. Especially when there are others who can do it."

Son took a deep breath and looked around. He didn't fully understand what his friend was trying to say, but he trusted his wisdom. He signaled to one of the townspeople that had helped prepare the meal the previous afternoon, then gave him instructions to recruit one more and continue the work of supplying the archers with arrows.

"But I don't know what to do," he confessed to Dulnear.

"Then gather together those who might," the man from the north advised.

Son looked over at Brunnlyn and Aesef, who had arranged the weapons from the barn into neat piles. He then saw Onclaid carry an armload of the enemy's weapons over to them, dropping them to the ground. "Will you come with me to speak with the others?" he asked.

"I will," Dulnear answered plainly.

Son was surprised by his friend's calm demeanor in the midst of the occasional flaming arrow that landed in the ground. On one occasion, when an arrow was going to strike him, he casually stepped left to avoid it.

The men assembled near the pile of weapons that Onclaid had built. The boy resisted the impulse to rub his hands together as anxiety clung to him like creeping ivy. "Thank you, friends," he began. "The northern opening we created seems to be serving its purpose as planned. But our people are getting fatigued. And, I didn't anticipate the flaming arrows from the west. I'm looking for suggestions from those of you with more experience in battle."

The four elder men looked at each other for a moment,

then back at Son. Onclaid raised his hand and began to speak, but was cut short by a blood-curdling scream from beyond the fiery wall.

Suddenly, the sound of steel clashing and shouting filled the air to the west, followed by a loud horn that sent chills through Son's spine.

"The Ohdium has arrived!" Argach could be heard shouting from where he was stationed.

Son looked into the sky to see that the flaming arrows coming from the other side had stopped. "I can't believe it!" he blurted.

"Believe it," Dulnear replied. "We've got to make a path for them."

Son looked back to the southern boundary where they had let Faymia and her friends in earlier. "Can you and Brunnlyn fetch the iron sheet we used earlier?" he asked.

"Of course," the man from the north nodded, and he and Brunnlyn ran off to retrieve the metal.

Son ran over to Argach, who was beaming at the sound of his countrymen fighting on the other side. "They came!" he exclaimed.

"I knew they would," Argach replied.

"And, by the sounds of it, they are making quick work of those archers!" Jarmour added.

Before much more could be said, Dulnear and Brunnlyn ran past them with the sheet of iron used earlier to allow Faymia and her friends through the flaming wall. Son, Argach, and Jarmour ran after them. When they dropped the metal over the fire to create a bridge, Son could see that the archers had all been defeated. However, a mob of slaver mercenaries was quickly approaching.

"Hurry!" Son called out to the Ohdium fighters. Many of them were on horseback, slashing down with their swords at the encroaching enemy.

Argach and Jarmour ran out to join the fray. When they saw their tribe's leaders, they shouted out.

"Into the circle!" Son shouted to the men from the Ohdium.

Dulnear and Brunnlyn ran out to fight off slaver fighters and encourage the new soldiers to enter the fiery circle. As they did, they noticed men fighting alongside the Ohdium warriors that looked more akin to farmers than soldiers. "Get Phel!" Dulnear yelled back to Son.

Within seconds, Son returned to the metal bridge with Phel.

"It's Aesef's men!" Phel announced. "Quickly!" he shouted out to them. "Over to this side!"

The farmhands immediately recognized Phel's voice and began making their way to the flaming barrier. Some of them were riding, some of them were running, and all of them carried makeshift weapons that more resembled hoes and rakes than swords and spears.

As the farmers flooded over the sheet of iron, the Ohdium fighters filed in behind them, fighting as they went. Finally, Dulnear and Brunnlyn crossed the bridge. As they pulled the metal away from the fire, several slavers tried entering the flaming circle with them, but the soldiers from the rift quickly put an end to them.

Son watched as Aesef, Phel, and the band of farmhands reunited. He was impressed by the loyalty that the workers held for Aesef. The looks in their eyes expressed that he was more than simply an employer to them, but a father figure and a leader. He hoped with his whole heart that he would be seen the same way one day. He heard the farmer express his gratitude to them and showed them over to the weapons piled near the burned-out barn.

The boy then turned toward the men from the Ohdium Rift and watched Argach and Jarmour embrace their respective tribal leaders and fill them in on the events thus far. Like Aesef, he noticed how Thuaid and Le'as led with genuine love for their people. He reckoned that love was the quality that made a good leader, and determined to get better at showing it. He went over to where the Ohdium chiefs were gathered and reintroduced himself.

"Thank you for coming to our aid," he said over the commotion.

Thuaid and Le'as both turned to the boy. With a smile on his face, Thuaid declared, "I remember you! You're a brave lad to stand up to those slavers!"

"Thank you," Son beamed.

"You made it!" another voice yelled. It was Faymia, who was now standing next to the boy with her hand outstretch.

"Lady Faymia!" Le'as called back. With a smile, he added, "What did you get us into?"

"What do you mean?" the woman answered with a giggle.

Thuaid took a small step forward. His expression was not jovial like his counterpart. "There are slaver mercenaries stretched eastward as far down the road as you can see from here," he began. "It is an army that outnumbers the whole lot of us four to one. Had we not discovered your band of farmhands, we may not have been able to take out those archers and make it in here to join you."

Son swallowed hard and did his best to suppress a tremble in his voice. "As far as you can see?" he muttered.

Thuaid's expression softened a bit as he looked into the boy's eyes. "As far as we could see," he repeated. He then paused for a moment, glanced at Faymia, then back toward Son. "But anyone with friends as loyal as you have, surely must have the strength to prevail. We are at your service."

Suddenly, the sound of metal clanging to the ground was all around them, and the flaming wall that surrounded them was suppressed all throughout its northern half. The northerners and townspeople who had been fighting all morning stepped back, and the flow of mercenaries they had been fighting stopped.

Son instinctively drew his sword and planted one foot behind him, as did Dulnear, Brunnlyn, and Onclaid. As his eyes adjusted to the gray morning light, he could see a vast crowd formed around Gale Hill. Some were dressed in the usual black dapper slaver apparel, while others appeared to be out-of-place commoners who were there hoping to gain a bounty. To the east, the boy could see a group of Greyus fighters, and there were several northerners scattered throughout the crowd.

Weakness filled his body. The reality that this day could be his last washed over him with a wave of unpleasant warmth. He watched as a small elderly man stepped forward, flanked by guards. He wore a black gown that touched the ground, and his gray hair and white beard were long and appeared to be tamed with too much oil.

"Ocmallum," Son heard Faymia whisper.

The boy gazed at the man who appeared on the scene like dark royalty. The memory of his encounter with him at Dorcadas rushed through his mind. He could once again feel the grip of his bony hands, and even smell his vile breath.

The slaves in the crowd bowed low to the slaver king, and the people parted to make way for him. Dulnear, Brunnlyn, Onclaid, and Faymia stepped in front of Son to protect him.

The boy wondered why no one was fighting the slavers. Perhaps they were frozen at the sight of such evil – or maybe it was something worse.

⸻

"I have to hand it to you, boy!" the twisted slaver king called out. His deep, raspy voice seemed to be felt as much as it was heard under the gloomy, gray morning sky. "I didn't think you had this many friends!"

Son felt overcome by fear. It was as if the air itself cowered beneath Ocmallum. He was grateful for his friends that stood between himself and the old man, but he knew it was a futile gesture. He wanted to shout out a response, but his lips felt frozen in place.

"You are not welcome here!" Dulnear shouted. "We will lay waste to you and that flotsam you call an army!"

Ocmallum stared deeply at Dulnear for what felt like hours. Finally, a sinister grin crawled over his face. He glanced back toward the crowd that accompanied him, and no less than ten northerners made their way to the front, standing directly behind him. "I brought some of your countrymen to play," he cackled. "And they have BOTH of their hands!"

Son shrank back further as he watched the giants draw their swords in intimidation. He felt death take a step closer to him as he considered that his Saor friends were outnumbered – and out-armed.

The slaver king cleared his throat and called out, "Boy! All of your friends are going to die today, but it doesn't have to be that way. Just step out from among them, and come with me."

For the first time, Son gave serious thought to surrendering to Ocmallum. He knew that the loss of his friends' lives would be too great to bear. Taking a deep breath, he stepped out in front of his protectors and shouted out to the old man, "And then what?"

"That's a good lad," the slaver king called back. "And then we both get what we want," he answered.

Son's head spun. He didn't understand what the old man meant. "I know you've come to kill me," he sputtered. "Everyone knows you've come to make an example of me after I pinned you down in Dorcadas."

Ocmallum's upper lip curled and he leaned his head forward. "Yes, Dorcadas. That was quite upsetting," he began. Then his face softened and he tilted his head slightly to the side. "But the more I thought about it, the more impressed I became by your bravery."

The boy felt a strange sensation in his stomach as he

heard the man's words. He stood silent, waiting to hear more.

"No one has ever come that close to killing me," the slaver king continued. "And you showed compassion on me, a trait that is rare in our world today." His eyebrows then pointed angrily toward each other and he added, "You should teach it to your friend who decided to lob a severed head over my castle wall."

"What?" Son blurted out, and he glanced back toward Dulnear.

"Perhaps," the northerner said quietly. "But do not listen to him. He is trying to deceive you."

"I'm telling the truth, boy!" Ocmallum rang out.

Son could hardly believe what he was hearing. He believed that his friend was moving away from his violent tendencies, and hoped that his choice of a mentor was not a poor one. He swallowed and attempted to keep up a stoney disposition. "So what!" he yelled back. "That still doesn't explain what you want with me!"

"Son," the old man said softly. "I know about your father. I'm very sorry to hear about his passing, and about his will."

The boy felt dizzy. He didn't know how Ocmallum could have known that information. Try as he might, he could not withdraw from his mind a response that was adequate.

"You see, boy," the slaver continued. "I have no children of my own and, if I had a son, I would want him to be like you. Come with me, and I will be the father you never had."

Son felt his chest heave and a tear came to his eye. His longing for a father was a void so great that even terrible evil might be overlooked to fulfill it. Dulnear had been a faithful figure in his life, but his recent gruesome actions left him disappointed. "And what will happen to my friends?" he asked.

"You have my word that I will not touch them," the old man answered. "In fact, the lovely Maren may come too, if she wishes. It would bring me great joy to have a daughter as well."

Son felt as if he had the world to gain by going with Ocmallum. He was an orphan, and so was Maren, whom he had sworn to care for. By going, they would have no financial worries, no fear for their safety, and no one would ever look down on them again. As he pondered this, he felt Maren's small hand clinging tightly to his. He looked down and saw her deep brown eyes staring up at him. "We can go," he said to her with a forced smile.

The young girl shook her head no, and a tear ran down her cheek.

"No? Why not?" the boy asked.

"Onaire," she answered, lip quivering as she nodded toward his sword.

Son held the hilt of his weapon up close to his face and gazed at its northern runes. He had forgotten that the blade even had a name. "Onaire," he repeated. "Blade of honor." Suddenly, a rush of memories charged through his mind. He remembered the impromptu Tismatayed ceremony where Dulnear accepted him as his own. He remembered the lessons he taught him about being strong and valorous. He was ashamed that he would, for even a moment, take the man for granted and consider forfeiting the ones he held dear for safety. "Thank you," he whispered to the girl, and wiped a tear from his eye.

"Okay," the young girl smiled as she squeezed his hand, then ran back to Phel, who was standing near the pile of weapons.

Son sheathed his sword and turned toward Dulnear. With gratitude swelling in his heart, he said, "I'm sorry. You have been more of a father to me than the man who raised me."

The man from the north knelt on one knee. Staring into the boy's eyes, he glowed. "Thank you, boy. I know that I disappoint at times. But know that you are more dear to me than words could ever say."

Son wrapped his arms around his friend's neck. With tears flowing from his eyes, he began to sob. "A million thanks, Dulnear."

The massive northerner cleared his throat awkwardly, and gently positioned Son an arm's length in front of him. "This moment means much to me," he began. "But we are surrounded by a sea of enemies, so we will need to continue this conversation later."

"Of course," Son smiled, embarrassed. "What do we do next?"

"Give the man his answer," Dulnear chuckled.

Son turned around and looked Ocmallum over. The old man somehow looked smaller and less threatening. Remembering all the times his mentor had riled his foes before a fight, he called out, "I'm sorry that your dusty old loins were never able to reproduce, but I'm not coming with you!"

A faint snicker could be heard throughout the crowd, and the slaver king's face grew red.

"We've been preparing for a long time to completely annihilate you, and I don't want all of that training to go to waste," Son added.

The old man's face turned sour and his eyes darkened. With a gesture to either side of him, a dozen Greyus warriors stepped out in front of him, clad in dark, weathered armor. "So be it, lad," he growled.

"Ha!" Dulnear barked. "We have destroyed the borb. Your clumsy fighters have lost their power."

"Have they?" Ocmallum snarled. Just then, a man carrying a large basket emerged from the crowd. He set the basket on the ground before the Greyus and ran back to his place. "I'm afraid you didn't destroy *all* of it," he cackled, and watched as the warriors took handfuls of the berries from the basket and greedily shoved them into their dark, stained mouths.

Dulnear nodded to Brunnlyn and Onclaid and the three of them stepped forward together as Son and Faymia jogged backward to join Maren.

The Greyus fighters moved toward the three northerners, meeting them in the middle of the field. They beat their chests and howled like animals, charged by the borb they had consumed.

"I only count twelve!" Dulnear shouted out to the slaver king. "I am insulted that there are not more!"

"Ever the jester!" Ocmallum called back. "For a useless Nairetu, you have a lot of confidence."

Hearing the old man call him a Nairetu, Dulnear's jovial demeanor turned quickly to seething anger. It was a northern word used to describe those who have had the dishonor of having their right hand removed, and was considered a punishment worse than death. Laying aside any further remarks, he simply grunted, "I will show you worse than dead." Then signaled to Aesef, who was standing nearby.

The old farmer ran out holding onto three large metal censers that resembled incense burners. He dropped them by the three northerners' feet, then ran back.

"Lovely!" Ocmallum shouted sarcastically. "Do you think a little incense is going to bless your battle?"

The three northerners picked up the censers by their attached chains and began to swing them back and forth. As they did, the smoke from within them filled the air around them.

"Whatever happens here today," Dulnear began, "you can be certain that you have lost your power." He then tossed his smoking metal ball so it landed amongst the dozen Greyus and announced, "And it is not incense. It is catnip."

Brunnlyn and Onclaid followed suit, and the armor-clad mercenaries began gasping and choking. Some fell to their knees and dropped their weapons. The three northerners ran up to the dozen warriors and began slashing them with speed and precision. In mere seconds, the field was littered with the dead bodies of the Greyus, and all became eerily silent.

"Where are your savage Greyus?" Dulnear asked. "Their corpses lay scattered in our field. You should go home before you join them."

Ocmallum's face contorted like a wrung-out rag. Nostrils flaring, he inhaled deeply, then bellowed, "Mai-ru!"

At his order, the dozen dark northerners who accompanied him stepped out from the crowd. They made their way to the center of the field and tossed the dead bodies of the Greyus warriors into the mob on either side of them.

As the other Saor brethren came alongside Dulnear and his companions, he reached into his coat and retrieved the mechanical hand Son had made for him. Latching it into place, he attached his sword to it and released a satisfying sigh. "Finally!" he shouted.

One of the dark-furred Mai-ru northerners stepped forward and glared at Dulnear. "What is this, one-hander?" he asked. "Are you going to fight us with that?" He then shot a glance to the men accompanying him and they snickered together.

Dulnear chose his words carefully. He knew that the other Mai-ru he met in the fields north of Dorcadas was not easy to kill, and that the challenge before him was immense. But something began to stir inside of him that only a warrior would appreciate. "Finally," he said again. "I have been in the south of Aun too long. My adversaries have been less than challenging. Now you are here to test my mettle and I feel born anew."

"Well, you are going to die anew," the man retorted. "We are greater in number, size, and strength."

"Perhaps," Dulnear began. "But I am Dulnear, son of Athnear, heir to the House of Stone and Blood, and you will die today." He then curled his upper lip and held his sword aloft. "Marhail!" he shouted.

"Marhail!" his fellow Saor repeated.

"That is an awful lot of confidence for a group of Nairetu," the dark northerner graveled. "But we have more steel."

Dulnear chuckled beneath his breath. "Do you know what else you have?" he asked.

"Oh, please tell me," the northern mercenary mocked. "Get out your last quip so we may commence with killing you."

"You have catnip smoldering at your feet," Dulnear explained. "And we have a kottur."

Suddenly, Verrox leaped over the Saor and began tearing flesh from the neck of the Mai-ru fighter. There were screams of terror as the other dark northerners leaped back to avoid being eaten by the catnip-fueled beast.

"Attack!" Ocmallum called out. "Everyone attack!"

There was a shout that shook the air as the slaver army pressed toward the field. The Laor townspeople, joined by the runaway slaves, rose to meet them.

## CHAPTER SIXTEEN

# WARRIORS REKINDLED

Not wasting any time, Dulnear rushed to attack the nearest Mai-ru warrior as Verrox tore the intestines from her prey. The warrior was visibly shaken by the sight of his companion being eaten by an enormous beast and for the first time, Dulnear actually believed that the slaver army could be defeated.

The man from the north shook his right arm to assure that his sword was firmly fixed in the device Son had made for him. Charged by the feeling of holding his sword right-handed again, he decided to forgo the usual verbal jousting and plunged his sword into the neck of his adversary with the kind of speed and precision that caused an onlooking Mai-ru to gasp.

Dulnear withdrew his sword from the man's body and didn't bother to watch it fall to the ground before turning to see two more of the dark northerners moving in quickly to attack. Once again dispensing with words, he quickly positioned himself to the side of the attacker to his right, forcing the man to either pivot or attack with his left hand.

Keeping his sword in his right hand, the man twisted his upper body to strike. Dulnear stepped sideways and thrust his blade into the man's ribcage, then kicked the Mai-ru's body into his partner, causing the man to lose balance. As he stumbled forward head-first, Dulnear brought his sword down forcefully and sent his head rolling toward Verrox, who began batting it around playfully.

"Hey, I want one of those!" Brunnlyn could be heard shouting over the noise.

"A head?" Dulnear yelled back. "Just cut one off!"

"No, a right hand!" Brunnlyn called.

Dulnear lopped off the right hand of the man he had just slain and tossed it toward his friend, who was currently engaged in a tense melee.

"Very funny!" Brunnlyn shouted. "If you are not busy, how about coming over here!"

"And giving you a hand?" Dulnear interrupted.

"You are despicable," Brunnlyn grunted.

---

Brunnlyn kicked the hand that was tossed to him. To his delight, it hit his opponent square in the face. The Mai-ru was taken aback with disgust, and Brunnlyn used the momentary distraction to strike him down.

The Saor leader looked around to see how his companions were faring in battle, and was pleased they were doing so well. He glanced to his right to see Dulnear jogging toward him.

"They are terrible at fighting from their left," his friend observed. "Simply keeping to their side gives us an edge."

"'Tis true," Brunnlyn agreed. "I never knew how weak our left hands were until I lost my right."

"I suppose us northerners have a weakness after all," Dulnear joked.

"Too many to count!" Brunnlyn concurred. Surveying the field once more, he noticed that the townspeople and runaway slaves were not faring quite as well as the Saor brethren. "There are just so many of them," he lamented.

Suddenly, a Mai-ru bloodied from battle stood before him. He held a sword in each hand and snarled like a rabid animal. His traditional fur coat had been torn off and his muscular arms were exposed.

Brunnlyn looked toward Dulnear to find that he was already battling another dark northerner nearby.

"Your friend is engaged and cannot help you," the Mai-ru sneered.

Brunnlyn studied the man as he stood, chest heaving, eyes wide, and lip curled. Holding his sword at the ready, he replied, "Then let us commence."

Unexpectedly, the Mai-ru kicked Brunnlyn square in the abdomen, sending him backwards, gasping for breath. Keeping his focus forward, he could see the man running toward him with both swords aloft.

Brunnlyn rolled sideways, desperately trying to regain his breath. The tip of the man's left sword caught his coat as he rolled, creating a long gash downward toward its hem.

Finally, he stood tall and was able to fill his lungs with air. Nostrils flared, he breathed deeply through his nose and every scent around him seemed to fill his senses at once. The damp ground, the burning trench, and the perspiration of men doing battle could all be detected in a single breath.

The bare-armed Mai-ru swung left, missing Brunnlyn, then followed through with a lunge with his right sword, which Brunnlyn blocked with a downward motion of his sword.

"If you surrender, I will kill you quickly and painlessly," the man taunted before slashing his left sword inward. It caught Brunnlyn on the right shoulder, knocking him over.

Brunnlyn found himself rolling left and used his body's momentum to continue rolling back to his feet. However, the pain in his shoulder told him that he did not recover from the strike uninjured. Knowing that his left-handed swordsmanship was probably going to be inadequate to defeat a two-handed swordsman, he thought of ways to disarm the man. Remembering how he had kicked the severed hand into his former opponent's face (which would one day be referred to as "The Hand Incident"), he spied a stone nearby and sent it flying with his foot.

The Mai-ru swung his right hand upward, knocking the stone into the distance and shook his head. "So, now we are throwing rocks, eh?" He then charged Brunnlyn once more. As he did, he extended his right sword, leveling it toward Brunnlyn's head.

Brunnlyn dropped low, spun around, and swiped upward, cutting deeply across the man's knuckles, nearly slicing off his fingers.

The Mai-ru dropped his sword and cursed. Growling, he spun right, thrusting his remaining sword toward Brunnlyn, who had stepped backward in anticipation.

The man tried in vain to recover his other sword but the cut was too deep, and his right hand did not have the strength to pick it up.

Brunnlyn tilted his head and glanced at the man's injured hand, then at the end of his own right arm. When the Mai-ru moved to attack again, he countered and removed the man's left hand above the wrist.

"Argh!" the man cried out. "What have you done?!"

Brunnlyn took pity on the northerner who could no longer hold a sword. Seeing him kneeling on the ground, unable to wield his weapon, he killed him quickly.

Dulnear blocked the Mai-ru's sword, but didn't anticipate his elbow. His opponent spun violently around and landed a blow against his chin, nearly dislocating his jaw. He stumbled back and took a fresh fighting stance while intently trying to keep his vision focused on the man.

"You are all going to die here today," the Mai-ru gloated.

Dulnear drew his sword back and gestured with his chin. "Look around you, forrador. You are the last of Ocmallum's northern parasites," he rasped. "We will cut down his mercenary rabble like winter grass."

A wry smile crept over the Mai-ru's face. "No. We are only the beginning," he wheezed. He then lunged forward with his sword.

Dulnear turned his body sideways and his enemy stumbled forward. He slashed his sword inward, cutting a deep gash into the back of the man's leg.

The Mai-ru growled and spun around, trying to keep his weight off his injured leg.

"What do you mean?" Dulnear sneered. "I have seen

Ocmallum's fortress. I burned his borb plantation to the ground. The Malitae refuse to fight with him. There is no one left."

The dark northerner let out a laugh that sounded akin to a wounded jackal. "I cannot wait to see your face when he arrives!" he jeered.

"When who arrives?" Dulnear demanded.

Suddenly, the Mai-ru rolled forward and sprang back to his feet, bringing his sword down hard toward Dulnear's head. Distracted by the man's ominous warning, he was unable to raise his sword to block in time.

Another sword swiped upward, knocking the Mai-ru's weapon upward.

"Keep your head in the battle!" Onclaid shouted as he stepped between Dulnear and his limping opponent. He shoved the man back, then drove his blade forward into the dark northerner's arm, causing him to groan in pain and drop his sword. Before the man could retrieve it, Onclaid cut a gash across his neck, dropping him to the ground.

Dulnear looked at his friend with an expression of disbelief. His eyebrows pushed downward as he thought about the Mai-ru's words. "Did you hear that?" he asked.

"First of all, you are welcome," Onclaid huffed. "And I am afraid I did not hear his words, as I was busy saving your life."

"How many Saor remain?" Dulnear asked.

"Seven, if you include yourself," Onclaid answered.

Dulnear scanned the battle taking place in front of him and gazed at the horizon for a clue to what the Mai-ru might have meant. "Hmmm... " he exhaled.

Brunnlyn jogged up next to Dulnear and Onclaid.

"Your beast is cleaning herself near the weapons pile," he announced. "'Tis a shame we cannot teach her to use a sword."

"A kottur with a sword may come in handy," Dulnear mumbled as he continued to watch for a new, more dangerous threat. "My opponent warned that a greater force is coming."

"Empty threats," Onclaid shot. "He was trying to shake you, and it worked."

"No," Dulnear argued. "There was much conviction in his voice. These were not the desperate last words of a defeated foe."

"Do you think Ocmallum was able to recruit the Malitae after all?" Brunnlyn asked.

"No. The Mai-ru said '*he* is coming.'" Dulnear explained. "But how could one man pose a threat to us?"

Brunnlyn pointed off into the distance. His mouth dropped open and his eyes grew wide as saucers. "Is that a King of the North? A genuine Tuais?" he gasped.

Dulnear squinted and rubbed his chin in dismay. "It cannot be," he muttered. "I thought they were made up by my mother to get me to behave."

Drawing closer was a giant man. He was as tall as four northerners. His head was wreathed in matted black hair, and his beard looked as if it was never trimmed. He was dressed in an assortment of rotting furs, and he wielded an oak tree that had been crudely carved into a sword.

"Cuonos," Onclaid cursed under his breath.

As the Tuais drew closer, the crowd that had been fighting parted to make way. The beast kicked or swatted anyone that stood in its way as its long, strong strides took it closer to Dulnear and his friends. Then, stopping in front of them, it cried out, "De!"

Dulnear made sure his sword was securely fastened in his mechanical right hand, then reached in his coat for a dagger with his left. "Marhail," he said to his companions.

"Marhail," they replied.

# THE REVENGE OF SEVUSS

S on took Maren by the hand and ran toward the southern edge of the field where the flaming wall was still burning. His plan was to hide the girl beyond Dulnear and Faymia's cottage, and return to fight with his friends.

"I don't want to hide!" Maren protested.

Son spun around and dropped to one knee. There was no time to comfort the young girl, but he knew that if he didn't, things might get even worse.

"I know you don't," he said, locking eyes with her. "And you are more brave than anyone else I know. But I need to know you're safe before I can fight as I should. And I need for you to say prayers for us."

Maren sighed a long sigh and relented. "Okay," she muttered. "But will you come get me if you need my sword?"

Son clenched his fist and placed it over his heart. "I promise," he declared.

The two began to drag a metal sheet over the flaming

trench. The fire seemed to be burning just as high as it was a few hours ago, and the boy wondered how long the oil would last.

Before they could create a bridge for themselves, a raspy voice spoke loudly from behind them. "Well look who it is!"

Son whipped his head sidewise to see a man dressed in fine black clothing. His gray and ginger hair looked like straw crudely glued to his scalp. Next to him stood a young boy dressed in similar garments. His brown hair was swept to the left, doing a poor job of covering the fact that his ear was missing.

Son immediately withdrew his sword, and Maren did the same.

"It's Sevuss!" Maren announced. "And Micah!"

"So, you remember us," Sevuss rasped. "Then you'll remember that you are my property." He then looked keenly at Son and added, "And after today, you will be the property of Ocmallum."

Son stepped forward and announced, "I'm afraid you came all this way to be disappointed." From where he stood, he could see the slaver army pressing in. His confidence was low, but he projected strength nonetheless.

Sevuss and Micah both drew swords of their own. Taking a small step forward, the man graveled, "We won't let you get away with what you did. First, we will take the girl's fingers." He held up his right hand and wiggled the stubby remains of the fingers Maren had cut off. "Then we will take her ears," he said as he gestured toward Micah.

Maren could be heard whispering, "Neck, knee, temple, foot, shin." She repeated the words quietly as her sword-wielding hand twitched.

"What's she saying?" Micah asked from snarled lips.

Son kept silent and carefully watched Sevuss's eyes for any indication of movement.

"Answer my boy," the slaver demanded. "What's she saying?"

Son remembered all of the battles he had fought alongside Maren. In vivid succession, he recalled fight after fight where the girl skillfully incapacitated fighters simply by reenacting the moves she observed Dulnear performing. Somehow, the young, defenseless girl he had rescued along the road to Blackcloth had become a warrior in her own right, and he had scarcely noticed. Suppressing a smile, he explained, "She is calling out the places on your body that she is about to seriously injure."

Sevuss laughed with a phlegmy cackle and looked over at his son, who did not look quite as confident. "We'll see about that!" he shouted, and he and Micah both charged Maren.

Instinctively, Son dove in front of the two attackers and cut Sevuss across the thigh as he did.

"Dad!" Micah shouted.

"Just kill that little brat!" the slaver replied. "I'll take care of this wastrel."

Son rolled to his feet and stood ready. His neck and shoulders were wound tight like steel and he had to will them to relax. "You shouldn't have allowed your desire for revenge to cloud your wisdom," he said. "Coming here was the last mistake you'll ever make."

"Big words from a little man," Sevuss retorted. "We'll see how confident you are when you're forced to bow before Ocmallum." He then brought his sword down toward the boy's shoulder.

Son raised his blade to block, but the force of the man's attack knocked him to the ground. The strike was followed by several kicks to his legs, shooting pain all the way up to his back. The slaver grasped the handle of his sword with both hands and moved it with a downward chop.

Son rolled out of the way to his right, then landed a jab to Sevuss's ribcage. The man grunted and grabbed his side but continued to advance.

As the two squared off once more, Son noticed another slaver mercenary running toward them. He positioned himself so that he would not have opponents on either side of him, then glanced at Maren, who was standing over Micah as he held his bleeding knee, foot, and shin. "We have company!" he called to the girl.

Maren darted to his side. By the time she was standing next to him, there were three more mercenaries approaching with weapons drawn.

"Get up, you good-for-nothing!" Sevuss yelled at his son. "We have them outnumbered three to one!"

As the slavers crowded in around them, Son knew there was no escape. It was fight or die for the two of them. Before he could issue any instructions to Maren, she was off like a wild animal cutting down slavers twice her size.

Son thought for a moment, then decided to approach the battle like Maren. He hoped that his body would remember his training with Dulnear and all of the time he spent practicing what he was taught.

He lunged forward and impaled Sevuss, dropping him in a lifeless pile to the ground. As he did, the other combatants stepped back for a moment. Son's heartbeat felt like heavy horse's hooves pounding the ground. Through its throbbing, he heard the men talking about his action in disbelief. In a moment, they pressed upon him with weapons raised high.

Son moved quickly, and his motions seemed automatic as he spun, kicked, and slashed his way through the men. At one point, he felt a knife cut across his shoulder blade, but he kept going as if a force greater than himself was empowering him.

Soon, Maren was at his side and they fought together as if the moment was choreographed the day before. But he was struggling to maintain his breath, and he could feel his muscles stiffening. Glancing north, he could see the Saor brethren battling a giant, and he knew Dulnear wouldn't be along to save him, so he kept fighting, as did Maren.

The brawl intensified as more attention was drawn toward them. Son felt death drawing closer, and he determined that he would take as many slavers with him as he could. Doing his best to keep one eye on Maren and one eye on his opponents, he noticed a strange commotion in the crowd.

A horrific sound filled the air. It was reminiscent of a tormented child's drawn-out wail of terror, and was followed by several shorter bursts of apparent agony.

Unexpectedly, a mercenary dropped from the sky in front of him, startling everyone. Son stepped away from the injured man, as did his attackers. To his left, the boy could see his enemies panicking and leaping away from a berserking animal.

"Earl!" Maren shouted.

The mule spun and kicked with its powerful legs, sending more men through the air. Its horrific braying reached a fever pitch that caused some of them to cover their ears.

Finally, the animal reached Maren, and everyone around watched in shock as she hopped on its back.

Son smiled as he considered the addition of Earl to their fighting efforts. He ran forward and began cutting down slavers while they were still stunned by what they had witnessed. Looking over to see how Maren and the mule were faring, he noticed that they were moving quickly away from the battle.

"Hey, where are you going?!" he shouted out.

"You'll be all right!" Maren called back.

"What??"

---

Son found himself fighting furiously as the slavers pressed in. With a wall of fire behind him, his only option was to keep doing battle or risk being consumed by the flames.

But there were too many of them.

The boy felt the pommel of a sword strike him across his temple and he stumbled sideways. There was raucous laughter and he felt a powerful kick to his ribs. A man punched him in the face, and he felt blood run down from his nose. He fell backwards onto his backside, but was able to keep himself from falling all the way to his back, and into the fire.

"Roast him!" someone called out.

"Look at all the men this runt killed. Take off his head!" another mercenary shouted.

The world around Son seemed to throb closer, then further away, and the angry faces brandishing weapons seemed unreal, as if he was dreaming. With death a breath away, he whispered a prayer and clutched his sword.

Just then, a strangely comforting thought flowed into the boy's mind. He felt that, in death, he would see his mother again. He closed his eyes and remembered her lovely face and the wonderful times they had together before she was taken to the hospital. Just as his body began to relax, an angry voice shouted from the crowd.

"Wait!" a man ordered. Pushing to the front of the mob, a slaver dressed in a fine black suit shoved and snarled at the mercenaries. "He is to be taken alive, you imbeciles!"

The man stood over Son. His dark, oiled hair hung in his face and he adjusted a pair of leather gloves over his manicured hands.

Son's thoughts returned to the situation at hand. He resumed his grip on his weapon and barked, "Death first!"

The slaver's lip curled and he wheezed a slithery laugh. "Oh no, boy. What you have waiting for you is far worse than death." He then ordered the men around him to take Son by his arms and legs and carry him to Ocmallum.

## CHAPTER EIGHTEEN
# THE FURY OF THE OHDIUM

S on twisted and writhed to break free from his captors. As he did, he heard them spewing the foulest obscenities, and occasionally, one of the men would spit on him. He let his head hang back, and he could see that his sword was still lying on the ground near the flaming barrier. He then lifted his eyes and could see that most of the battle had shifted its focus around his location, with the exception of the northerners battling their enormous opponent.

"Let me go!" the boy shouted in vain. "Put me down!"

"It's over, kid," the man dressed in black cackled. "Soon you'll be kneeling at the feet of the slaver king." He then chuckled and added, "You really should have taken him up on his offer. You would have been carried out of here like royalty."

Son closed his eyes and tried to make sense of all that had taken place that morning. He knew that the promises of safety and care from Ocmallum were all lies. He knew that such promises have always been used by the powerful to manipulate those who were not. Perhaps his refusal to live by the ways of such men is what infuriated the slaver king so much. The dark ruler had no tolerance for self-sufficiency, and abhorred contentment. Son decided that, whatever he would face that day, he would not fear it, but rather go through it with as much grace as he could draw upon from the Great Father. He let his body relax, and he allowed the men to take him where they wished.

"That's right," the man in black grunted, leading the morbid parade. "There's no point in resisting. It will all be over soon."

The boy then heard the man make a strange gurgling sound. He opened his eyes to see what he was doing. There was an arrowhead emerging from one side of his neck, and a feather protruding from the other side. The man grasped at his neck, then fell to his knees.

The men holding Son dropped him in panic and drew their weapons. The boy couldn't help but notice how their ugly bravado so quickly turned to fear and confusion. Another arrow flew through the air, striking one of them, then another.

Son took the opportunity to run back and fetch his sword. Glancing east, he could see Maren atop the great beast Verrox, steering her into battle. Sitting behind her was Phel, launching arrows at the slavers. Running beside them was Aesef, wielding his massive sword. The boy was fairly certain he saw Earl following a ways behind them as well.

Seeing his friends plow into the mass of mercenaries, his vigor was renewed and he joined them. As he did, he noticed that the army's first inclination was to retreat north, but something pushed them back toward the south, engaging them fully in battle. Some of the townspeople were now standing alongside of him, and they fought with great tenacity.

"Keep pressing in!" Son encouraged the Laor locals and runaway slaves around him. "We've already done more damage than they anticipated, and we have them scared!"

"You have no idea!" a familiar voice called out.

"Henry!" Son shouted back. "I'm surprised you're still alive!"

The barkeep made an odd expression and gazed at the boy. "What?" he croaked.

Immediately regretting the words he chose, Son answered, "I'm surprised you're leaving any alive! Fight on!"

"Okay!" Henry shouted, and he fell in behind Verrox, taking any slavers trying to attack the beast from its backside.

Suddenly, the enemy shifted its attention to the north once more, and a battle cry could be heard from a distance. Men began to run east over the bridges Ocmallum had created over the flaming wall. When Son realized what was happening, he recruited a couple of the runaway slaves and they began removing the sheets of metal to keep the slavers inside the ring of fire with them.

---

Faymia was exhausted. The mass of mercenaries in front of her seemed to remain the same number regardless of how many she and the Ohdium forces took out.

"I can see the boy, and that enormous cat!" Thuaid

called down. He sat atop his horse hacking at the any slaver who dared to come near.

"I see him too!" Le'as shouted, also from his horse.

Faymia continued to fight on, wishing she had her horse as well. Her legs were tired, and the fatigue of fighting continually since the dark hours of morning meant that concentration was a constant effort. She had long since run out of arrows and now fought with a sword in her right hand and a dagger in her left. Fortunately, the northern steel her husband supplied her with cut with astonishing effectiveness through the shabby armor that her opponents wore, if they happened to have the luxury of wearing armor.

"On your left!" Argach shouted.

The woman glanced over just in time to see a slaver drawing back his sword to strike her. Pivoting so that she was leading with her right hand, she thrust her sword forward to eliminate the man. But as soon as his limp form hit the ground, two more mercenaries were upon her.

As the attacker to her left swiped his blade toward her she raised her forearm, with her dagger pressed up against it, to block. At the same time, the other man came in with a lunge from his sword. She disarmed the man with a rapid strike of her blade, then felt a kick to her left leg as the first mercenary swung his boot at her.

Spinning left, Faymia plunged her dagger into the chest of the second attacker, then pushed her sword into the belly of the first. They landed on the ground leaning on each other, but were now replaced by three more slavers.

"It's the woman!" someone yelled.

Faymia could hear that the mercenaries around her were telling each other to press in.

"That's the northerner's wife," another observed. "We can use her to get the boy to surrender."

Faymia didn't know how much longer she could hold out against an attack by so many. She took a deep breath, strengthened her grip on her weapons, and began to plot her defense. Before she could even raise her sword, she could see that Thuaid had dismounted and was standing to her right. She nodded toward him and he gestured to her left. When Faymia looked to her left, she could see that Le'as was standing on the other side of her.

"We are with you, Lady Faymia," Thuaid declared.

Faymia was impressed by the skill the two chiefs possessed. From the corner of her eye, she could see Le'as swiftly cut down mercenaries until they began to give pause before charging in. She was not expecting such brutality from a man she considered to be rather meek.

Unfortunately, the other Ohdium ranks were not having as much success as the chiefs and their aides. The slavers fought with less dignity, and their fighting often included cheap moves and underhanded tactics to gain an edge. They often resembled savages, swinging wildly to overwhelm their opponent.

"I think this is going quite well," she heard Argach chime as he pulled his blade from the belly of a slaver. He was now standing to the right of Thuaid.

"Agreed," the Ohdium chief replied. "We may be burning bodies by dinner."

Faymia found their exchange rather morbid, but was grateful for their optimism. "I hope you're right," she added.

As the battle raged on, the woman noticed a shift in the

enemy's attention. Suddenly, one of the northern Mai-ru emerged from the crowd. He was bleeding from his leg, and he growled as he withdrew his sword.

"Looks like your ferocious beast left one behind," Le'as observed.

Before anyone had a chance to reply, the wounded northerner was bringing his blade down upon Faymia. "You shall die!" he shouted. "Then your husband, the boy, and the little brat," he added.

The woman raised her sword to block, but was knocked to the ground by the brute strength of the massive fur-clad northerner. Argach stepped around Thuaid and plunged his sword into the enemy's ribs.

Howling in pain, the man struck Argach with a massive backhanded fist, sending him flying backward. As he reeled on the ground, mercenaries ran toward him to finish the job the Mai-ru had started.

Immediately, Thuaid ran to his assistant to protect him, and made quick work of any slavers who came near.

Le'as and Jarmour were now attacking the northerner from the other side, drawing his attention from Faymia. Once the woman had recovered, she joined in the attack. With surprising speed, the large Mai-ru fought back with his massive sword.

Once Argach had recovered, he shouted and ran into the fray. When he reached the northerner, he hacked at the savage fighter's wounded leg. In pain, the giant dropped to one knee. As he did, he withdrew a dagger from his pocket with his left hand, threw his arm backward, and plunged the blade into Argach's neck. He then withdrew it just as quickly.

"Noooo!" Faymia screamed as she watched her friend stumble backwards holding his neck. She lunged forward, stabbing the northerner in the abdomen. He dropped his sword and fell backward, sitting on the ground.

When she reached Argach, Thuaid was already kneeling at his side. The mercenaries were watching from a distance as if they weren't sure what to do.

"It's okay," Argach whispered as blood streamed from the wound in his neck.

"My friend," was all Thuaid could say as he watched the light in his faithful servant's eyes grow dim.

Faymia's body shook as she watched the man who had been so kind to her slip into eternity. She felt an involuntary compulsion to sob, but held it back. "He's gone," she whispered to herself.

---

Thuaid stood to his feet. His face was red, and a tear ran down his cheek. His voice trembled as he declared, "The northerner must die!"

Regret and sadness poured into Faymia's body. When she arrived at the Ohdium a few days ago, they were enjoying a time of peace and harmony like they hadn't known in a generation. Now they were here dying in a battle that was not theirs. "I'm sorry!" she cried.

The highground chief seemed to give no notice to Faymia as he marched back toward the Mai-ru northerner fighting off Le'as and Jarmour. Some of the other Ohdium soldiers were engaged as well but even with a wounded leg, the giant was a formidable opponent.

Faymia gripped her sword, swallowed hard, and rallied herself as she turned to follow Thuaid against the northerner. As a slaver mercenary ran to cut her off from her path, she impaled him and withdrew her sword from his body before he even had a chance to raise his weapon against her.

While the Mai-ru was still engaged with Le'as and Jarmour, Thuaid repeated Argach's attack against the brute's wounded leg. Again, the warrior howled in pain and flung his dagger-wielding left hand backward.

Anticipating this, Thuaid stepped left and brought his blade down hard, removing the northerner's hand completely. While the man paused in shock, the chief plunged his sword deep into his foe's belly. The Mai-ru dropped his sword, grabbed the chief's, and snarled like a cornered animal. Thuaid forcefully pulled it away and stepped back, watching him curse as he dizzily stared back, then fell to the ground.

At the sight of the black northerner falling, the other mercenaries stepped back, and some turned their attention elsewhere. However, the soldiers from the Ohdium continued to press in, refusing to let up their attack. As they did, Thuaid ran over to Le'as and Jarmour to discuss their next move, and Faymia followed.

The woman stood to the side and saw the sympathy in the lowground chief's eyes as he fought back a tear to offer his condolences. "I'm so sorry about Argach," he offered as he placed his hand on Thuaid's shoulder.

"As am I," Jarmour added. "He was respected throughout the Ohdium."

"Thank you," the highground chief replied. "But there will be time for mourning when the battle is over."

"It appears that the soldiers we brought with us and the sword-wielding folks from Laor are making headway against the mercenary army," Le'as began.

Faymia surveyed the field. She could see that her husband and a couple of the Saor brethren were very much occupied with the brutal King of the North. Her eyes widened, and she wanted with everything to run to him and fight alongside him. "Perhaps we can help put an end to their mammoth northerner," she suggested.

"No!" a gravelly voice shouted from behind Thuaid, and a large dagger emerged from the chief's chest.

Faymia leapt back to see the Mai-ru thrusting his dagger into the chief's back, lifting him off the ground. She darted forward and cleaved off his right hand with her sword. Spinning left, Le'as attacked with an outward slash of his sword, slicing halfway through the northerner's neck as he was propping himself up with the bloody stump of his left arm.

The Mai-ru attempted to speak, but could not. Blood gushed from his neck, and he collapsed to the ground. Le'as chopped down and removed his head with a shout, then turned toward his friend, who was holding the sharp end of the northern dagger protruding from his chest.

"My friend!" Le'as cried. He dropped his sword as he rushed to catch the highground chief before he fell backward.

Faymia felt another rush of sadness come upon her for involving the Ohdium chiefs in the battle. She knelt beside

Le'as as he held his friend and wept. Jarmour joined them, and together they comforted Thuaid as he breathed his final labored breaths.

The highground chief turned his head toward Le'as and gave him a strange smile. "Look at us," he whispered. "Never in my life did I imagine that I would die fighting alongside of you."

"Nor did I," Le'as said in return.

"In the end," Thuaid continued through labored exhales, "It is better to die fighting with you than against you. Lead well, my friend. Continue to unite the Rift."

"I will," Le'as choked. His chest heaved, and he closed his eyes tightly as tears flowed down his face.

"And you, Lady Faymia," Thuaid groaned as he turned his eyes toward her. "Do not think that you did some injustice by bringing us into the battle."

The words he spoke were like a warm hand on her shoulder. Faymia slowly exhaled the sorrow she was feeling as she wept.

"The plague upon Aun has already experienced a devastating blow on this field today, and I am honored beyond words to have been a part of it. I am right where I need to be," he said. "The fields of eternity are becoming clearer to me," he continued as he turned his eyes toward the sky. "The Great Father awaits, and I can hear the song of my life floating through the air."

Faymia watched as her friend and ally ceased breathing and his eyes were emptied of life. The three of them lowered Thuaid's body to the ground and looked at each other in disbelief. Finally, Le'as asked, "What is next, Lady Faymia?"

The woman gazed toward the battle happening directly in front of her, then at the melee taking place between the Saor brethren and the King of the North. "We have to help my husband defeat that ogre of a northerner," she gulped.

## CHAPTER NINETEEN

# THE KING OF THE NORTH

"You go for the legs, and I will go for the belly," Dulnear instructed his companions.

"And how do you plan on reaching his belly?" Onclaid asked.

"I will be able to reach it once you have disabled his legs," Dulnear answered.

"I suppose you are referring to those massive tree trunks as legs," Brunnlyn added.

"Do you have a better plan?" Onclaid asked through clenched jaw.

Dulnear surveyed the battlefield, rubbing his chin. The other Saor were either preoccupied, injured, or worse. Defeating the Tuais was going to take a miracle, but failing was not an option.

"De!" the King of the North bellowed out again.

"Apparently, he wants us to die," Brunnlyn quipped as he adjusted his grip on the hilt of his sword.

Suddenly, the giant swung his massive wooden sword

left, then right, hurtling half a dozen slaver mercenaries through the air. "De!" he shouted.

"Why do they always do that?" Onclaid asked.

"What? Kill their own to intimidate us?" Dulnear answered. "Thank you for doing us a favor, tree man!" he shouted at the monster. He then glanced at his companions to see if they were amused by his heckling.

"Tree man?" Brunnlyn chortled. "Is that the best you can do?"

"I did not hear you cracking wise," Dulnear retorted.

Suddenly, the Tuais took a massive step forward and raised his oaken sword above his head. "DE!!" it belched.

"Okay, let us do this!" Onclaid shouted, and the three northerners shouted as they rushed to meet their attacker.

Brunnlyn ran left and slashed at the giant's leg, and Onclaid ran right to wound its foot. Dulnear remained a few steps behind, waiting to attack its abdomen, but his two friends seemed to be nothing more than nuisance to the monster as it swatted them away.

The man from the north bobbed left, then right, hoping he could find a way to slice at any part of the Tuais's exposed skin. When Onclaid came sailing through the air toward him, he had to duck so he would not be bowled over.

Suddenly, the giant grabbed Dulnear around the waist and lifted him off the ground. Seeing his opportunity, Dulnear plunged his dagger into its hand.

"Yowww!" the beast cried, and tossed him back to where he was standing a moment ago.

Dulnear landed on his back. With the wind knocked out of him, he dropped his dagger. He staggered to his feet just in time to rejoin his companions who were now moving back toward the Tuais with a little more caution in their steps. "New plan!" he shouted. "Attack his left leg together, and I will cut him from behind."

Onclaid and Brunnlyn moved closer to the giant's leg, but found it difficult to do much more than avoid the massive boot that was now trying to stomp on them. However, it provided Dulnear with the opportunity he needed while it was distracted. He got up underneath the beast, partially covered by the patchwork of furs. He sheathed his dagger, hoping to use his free hand to scale its rear leg and stab it in its side. However, he was suddenly overcome by the immense stench of the Tuais.

"Like a punch in the face!" Dulnear gagged.

"Any time now!" Onclaid shouted as he narrowly avoided being cut in half by the tip of the Tuais's wooden sword.

Dulnear snorted as he took a deep breath and held it in. He quickly climbed up the giant's right leg, going inside its rancid coat. Clinging to its hip with his legs, he drew back his sword. Since he was under the beast's coat, he was unable to draw his weapon back as far as he preferred. He pushed the blade as far as he could into its side, but it only seemed to penetrate a layer of fat.

"Hey!" the King of the North shouted. He then moved his sword to his left hand and swept back against his side with his right.

Dulnear felt the huge hand knock against him. It dislodged his legs from their perch, and he was now dangling by the submerged sword that he was unable to release. Suddenly, the smelly coat he was under came flying off, exposing him. The giant grabbed him by the legs, pulling the sword from his side, and tossed him through the air.

Once again, the man from the north was on his back gasping for air. Staring up into the cloudy gray sky, he prayed for strength to continue the battle.

"Get up!" a familiar voice called out.

Dulnear sat up and looked around. His friends were still engaged with the Tuais. Onclaid was dodging its sword, and Brunnlyn was trying not to be swatted by its putrid fur coat.

"Get up!" the voice rang out again.

Dulnear glanced to his right and could see Faymia running toward him, followed by Le'as and Jarmour. She stopped a stone's throw from her husband. Her quiver was now filled with an assortment of her own arrows and the enemy's. She withdrew one and fired it toward the giant.

"De!" the Tuais yelled out, and took a massive step toward her.

---

Dulnear leapt to his feet and ran toward Faymia. By the time he arrived, Brunnlyn and Onclaid had already joined her. She and her companions from the Ohdium were firing arrows at the King of the North, but their attack was short-lived as the giant swung his enormous wooden sword at them.

Once again, Brunnlyn and Onclaid rushed in to attack the beast's legs, trying to find a way to bring injury.

"What are you doing here?!" Dulnear shouted to his wife.

"I'm trying to help!" she shouted back.

"Go help Son!" he ordered.

"He and Aesef's men have things under control," she retorted. "In fact, they've trapped them in the wall of fire so they won't escape."

Dulnear furrowed his brow and turned his attention to the melee surrounding Son and Maren. He then stared at Faymia. "Where is Ocmallum?" he asked.

"I don't know. Perhaps he fled," she answered.

Before Dulnear had a chance to say anything further, the giant's fur coat came flying through the air and crashed into the two of them, sending them sailing backward.

"Heads up!" Brunnlyn shouted as he ran toward them.

"You're supposed to say that BEFORE we get hit!" Faymia grunted as she accepted the northerner's help to get to her feet.

"Better late than never," Brunnlyn replied.

"No, not really," the woman said.

Dulnear stood up and quickly surveyed the field once more. The remaining slaver mercenaries had now diverted their attention toward Son and Maren, and the Tuais was all that remained in front of him. However, he knew that the beast was more than a match for himself and his companions. "Okay, keep firing," he instructed. "Perhaps if you three archers distract him, the three of us northerners can open his belly. Especially now since his coat is off. Aim for his hand, and maybe he will drop his weapon."

Faymia, Le'as, and Jarmour fired arrows at the giant. They were able to penetrate its skin wherever it was exposed, but it seemed only to agitate the beast. As it moved toward putting an end to their attack, Brunnlyn and Onclaid went to work on its legs once more. Both of them managed to stab it above its boots this time, causing it to howl.

Dulnear quickly scurried up the side of the Tuais and stabbed it in its side. It howled again, and Dulnear jumped to the ground before taking another swat from its enormous hand. When the beast's attention moved toward the northerners at his feet, Dulnear climbed up and stabbed it again.

Just as the man from the north began to believe that their plan was working, he noticed that the arrows were no longer flying. He hopped back to the ground and saw that Faymia and her friends were out of ammunition. They had drawn their swords and were now running to join him. "Stay back!" he called out, but they were unable to hear him amidst the chaos.

He climbed back up the Tuais's back as it reached down and took hold of Brunnlyn, tossing him toward the house. From his vantage point, he could see Son and Maren making their way over to help fight the giant too. "No!" he said to himself, and plunged his sword into its shoulder.

The Tuais grabbed Dulnear and held him high in the air. He then dropped him to the ground and stomped on him. The man from the north felt several of his bones break beneath the force of the monster's foot. He felt another blow from its foot and he slid along the ground, stopping in the same place he landed the last time he was thrown.

He could hardly lift his head as he watched Faymia nimbly climb up the monster and stab him in the abdomen.

It roared once more, grabbing Faymia and throwing her past her friends from the Rift.

Dulnear's heart turned sick as he watched his wife land on her side in the distance. There was no movement from her, and he was unable to go to her.

With agonizing pain, he turned his head toward the Tuais, who was swinging his sword at Son. The boy moved quickly, but was unable to get close enough to strike the giant.

Maren dismounted Verrox and tended to Faymia, who was still unmoving on the ground. The giant cat ran up the side of the King of the North, digging its claws into him.

"De!" the Tuais shouted again, clearly in pain from the claws of the kottur. It frantically reached around in an attempt to peel the cat off of him, but it found its way onto his shoulder and began scratching at his neck.

Now bleeding freely from his neck, the creature grabbed Verrox by the nape of her neck and slammed her to the ground before kicking her into the distance.

Dulnear prayed that the battle they were fighting would not be in vain, then lowered his head to the ground. The world around him grew dark and cold, and he could feel what little strength he had left evaporate into the afternoon air.

***

"Dulnear!" a desperate voice cried out.

Opening his eyes, the man from the north could see Brunnlyn standing over him. His friend knelt down and examined his broken body.

"It is over," Dulnear groaned. "Leave me and tend to Faymia. Get her, Son, and Maren to safety."

"No!" Brunnlyn pleaded. "We must finish what we started, or this was all for nought."

"Standing for what is right is never for nought," the man from the north whispered.

"But we are so close," the Saor leader contested. "The kottur nearly bled the King of the North to death."

The thought of the animal that had followed him from Tuas-arum gave Dulnear pause. He agonizingly lifted his head and surveyed the field once more. In the midst of the fruitless fight between the giant, Son, Le'as, Jarmour, and Onclaid, he noticed the censers filled with catnip lying on the ground. They were no longer burning, and had long since been batted to the side by Verrox. "Take my coat off," he said to Brunnlyn.

"What?" the fellow northerner croaked. "The pain would be unbearable."

"Then do it quickly, and be as gentle as possible," Dulnear instructed.

Brunnlyn began to tug at the left sleeve of the fur coat. As he did, excruciating pain shot through Dulnear's body with every motion, and he willed himself to not lose consciousness. He then disconnected the sword from his right arm so he could get the other arm out of the sleeve.

Dulnear noticed a tear forming in the corner of Brunnlyn's eye as he carefully pulled the coat out from underneath his limp body. "It is okay," he comforted his friend. "Now reattach my sword."

Brunnlyn dutifully did as he was told, though tears now flowed down his face.

Dulnear laid there and stared at the sky for a moment. The last season of his life ran like a stage play through his mind. He recalled leaving Tuas-arum to seek out a more peaceful life. He remembered meeting Son for the first time in the pub on the road to Blackcloth. He remembered his unpleasant first impressions of Faymia, falling in love, and his eventual marriage to her. He recalled the bravery of Maren, and how she had become like a daughter to him. As the images presented themselves, a tear now escaped his eye, and he was overwhelmed with a flood of gratitude. "Now," he said to Brunnlyn. "Reach into my coat pocket."

His friend reached deep into the pocket of his fur coat and felt around. Finding what was lying at the bottom, he withdrew a handful of berries. "What are you doing with these?" he asked.

"Please," Dulnear groaned. "Place the borb in my hand."

"But... " Brunnlyn stammered. "You will die."

"I am already dead," the man from the north replied. "Please, give them to me."

Brunnlyn placed the berries in Dulnear's hand and closed his fingers over them. "I am with you," he murmured.

Dulnear covered his lips with his left hand and let the borb drop into his mouth. As he chewed them, a thin line of black ran from the edge of his bottom lip.

A strange energy began to fill his broken body. He balled his left hand into a fist and he sat up. His heart raced. He felt as if he could take off running and never stop. The world around him took on an extreme focus and contrast. Each sound and smell seemed to fuel an agitation in him, and he wanted to strike out. He suddenly felt no pain. Each ache was replaced by anger and aggression.

"Can you hear me?" Brunnlyn asked.

"Aye," Dulnear answered in a low growl.

"Can you stand?" his friend stuttered.

"Stay behind me," Dulnear warned. "And tell the rest to do the same."

Dulnear ran like a tornado toward the giant, growling like a rabid animal.

His friends stood staring in disbelief until Brunnlyn called out, "Help him!"

The King of the North swung his sword toward Dulnear, but he ran around it like a gazelle, rolled through its legs, and climbed up its back once again.

Midway up its back, the beast reached behind him and swatted the man from the north, nearly knocking him back to the ground. Dulnear quickly regained his foothold and made his way to the Tuais's left shoulder. Quickly, he plunged his sword into the giant's neck, nearly piercing its jugular vein.

"De!" the beast howled, and it reached up to pull Dulnear from its shoulder.

The northerner was knocked from his perch and was now dangling by his sword that was embedded in the giant's neck. The Tuais continued to grope blindly for Dulnear until it howled in pain and gave up.

Dulnear looked down and could see Brunnlyn and Onclaid stabbing at the beast's legs, distracting it for him.

He swung himself back up upon its shoulder and dislodged his sword from its neck. It bellowed again and shook. This time, Dulnear rolled down the beast's back but managed to grab ahold of its shirt before falling too far. He climbed onto its right shoulder and prepared to attack once again.

Seeing the wounds Verrox had made, Dulnear knew exactly where to strike. He thrust his sword into the neck of the giant and began to move it back and forth in a sawing motion.

"De!" the beast cried out and hit Dulnear with the back of its hand.

The man from the north felt his leg break but held his ground upon the massive shoulder, thanks to the borb. Soon, blood was pouring from the Tuais's neck, flowing down the front of its shirt.

Dulnear pulled his sword from the beast's neck and held on as it stumbled backward, then fell to its knees. He knew it would only be a matter of time before it fell, so he leapt onto the ground.

Feeling his fractured leg snap completely, he limped forward as fast as he could before the giant fell on him. Before he knew it, the beast's arm was covering him and he could not break free. He fell to his knees as extreme pain slowly began to envelop his body and the effects of the borb began to fade.

"Dulnear!" he heard one of his friends cry out.

"It is done," the man from the north whispered. He closed his eyes and hoped to lose consciousness before the pain overtook him.

"Get him out!" Son shouted. He didn't know why he was shouting since the Saor brethren, Le'as, and Jarmour were already hard at work pulling his friend out from under the Tuais's massive arm.

Upon removing Dulnear, they carefully dragged him away from the fallen monster, resting him on his back. Son rushed to his side and knelt beside him. At Dulnear's other side knelt Faymia and Maren.

Son's heart beat as if it had been set on fire. The ground itself seemed to move and he held onto his friend's arm just above the metal attachment he had made for him. "Dulnear!" he began to sob.

The man from the north turned his head slightly toward the boy, wincing in pain. He opened his eyes to mere slits and whispered, "Son. You are here."

"Yes, I'm here," the boy replied through his tears. "Please stay with me."

"I am afraid I cannot," his friend groaned. "I have fought my last battle." He then drew a labored breath and continued. "Son, I must say thank you."

"Thank you?" the boy gasped. "For what?"

"You have blessed me in countless ways," the man said. "I do not know what I would have done had I not met you along the road to Blackcloth."

Son willed himself to not fall into uncontrollable sobbing. Gaining his composure, he said, "It is I who am blessed."

"You have come so far," Dulnear continued. "I am incredibly proud to have had you at my side. Do you remember what I said about coal and diamonds?"

"Yes," the boy nodded.

"You have become so bright," the man from the north wheezed. "I have never met another like you."

The man from the north then turned his gaze toward Maren and said, "And you, my daughter."

"Uh-huh," the young girl chirped through teary eyes.

"I wish the rest of the world could see you as I do," Dulnear whispered through a weakening smile. "You are strong like an elk, and twice as fast. And may just be the smartest child I have ever met. I only wish that I could be here to see you grow."

"Thank you," the young girl said as she closed her eyes as if to allow the words to wash over her.

Dulnear then turned his eyes toward Faymia. With her left hand in his, the two simply gazed into each other's eyes for a moment. "I love you," he finally spoke.

"I love you," the woman replied as tears flowed freely down her cheeks.

"If you were to count how much I love you, and the many ways you have changed my life, it would outnumber the sands on the seashore," the man said, holding her gaze.

Faymia laid her head on her husband's chest, weeping. "And if you were to count how much I love you," she began, "it would outnumber the sands on the seashore, the steps from here to Tuas-arum, and the clouds in the sky."

Son watched as Faymia's head would rise and fall with each of Dulnear's labored breaths. There were a thousands words he wanted to say in that moment, but he could not untangle his thoughts enough to utter a single one.

Finally, the man who was a father to him in ways his own could never have been breathed one last full breath, exhaled, and was gone.

## CHAPTER TWENTY

# RISING SON

A s Son wiped his tears, he noticed the shape of three figures out of the corner of his eye. A feeling in his stomach told him to be on guard. He sprang to his feet and, though he had no recollection of drawing it from its scabbard, he was holding his sword with a steel grip.

"Well then," Ocmallum called out as he and his two elite guardsmen drew closer. "I see the pompous northerner has received his comeuppance."

The old man seemed somehow taller and broader. His once-arthritic hands looked strong and sure. The guards at his left and his right were eerily silent and still, and their eyes never blinked.

The words of the slaver king angered the boy. Both tears and rage threatened to burst forth from him and he willed himself to maintain a stoney composure. "You are defeated," he spoke with a low growl in his voice. "Your army is beaten and your giant has fallen. Go home, and never lure another into slavery again."

A wry smile crept across the old man's face. He pointed his sword at Son and snickered, exposing his gray and black teeth. "This was never about my army," he began. "This is about you and me, and it's time for me to collect your head for my trophy case." Laughing, he added, "And I might as well take that sorry excuse for a northerner's head too. He won't be needing it."

Son's blood boiled. Searching for a retort, he stood frozen until he noticed his friends standing by his side.

"I'm with you," Maren said, holding a dagger.

"So am I," Faymia added.

"As are we," Brunnlyn declared.

"Thank you," Son replied.

"Ah, the last stand. How lovely," Ocmallum taunted. "Once again, you don't know who you're dealing with, or what you're dealing with."

Son took a deep breath and slid his right foot back to fortify his stance. "I believe you are the one who doesn't know," he said. Then glancing left and right toward his friends, he added, "I'll take the old man."

"Leave the guards to us," Brunnlyn instructed, and before anyone could take a breath, Son's friends were pressing back against the guards, leaving him alone with Ocmallum the slaver king.

Son lunged forward, thrusting his sword toward the old man's abdomen. To his surprise, Ocmallum moved with startling speed, sidestepping the attack and countering by disarming the boy and knocking his sword to the ground.

"What's the matter, boy?" the slaver king asked. "Did you forget how to fight?"

Son couldn't believe what had just happened. The old man he had done battle with in Dorcadas seemed to be replaced by someone much more formidable. He felt his hands begin to shake as he inched backwards.

"Let's give that another try," Ocmallum offered. "I'll step back and let you fetch your sword."

Son watched as the slaver king stepped back three paces, then made a broad gesture toward his sword lying on the ground. He knew he could not trust the man, but saw no hope in defeating him without his weapon.

Leaping forward, the boy grabbed his sword, then rolled left, narrowly missing the slaver king's downward attack. He sprang to his feet and took several steps back as he struggled to believe what he was seeing.

"The borb berry is a funny thing," Ocmallum began. "Ingested raw, it brings on unchecked aggression. But processed with a few herbs and roots, it simply makes a man stronger and faster."

Fear began to gnaw at Son as he considered what the man had said. Every muscle in his body contracted, and he held his sword with stark-white knuckles. Gritting his teeth, he attacked again. This time, the slaver king blocked each blow, then caught the boy's nose with the back of his sword-wielding hand.

Son flew back a few steps, then glanced down to see the blood from his nose flowing freely to the ground. Wiping his upper lip with his sleeve, his mind worked furiously to formulate a plan to defeat the old man. "It doesn't surprise me that you would cheat to defeat a boy smaller than you!" he shouted.

Ocmallum's expression changed from one of amusement to mock repentance. "Oh no! How could I?!" he retorted. "Spare me your sermons on fairness and honor, boy! You do not become the slaver king by operating by the rules of the masses." The man then stepped toward Son and swiped his sword over the boy's head.

When Son flinched, Ocmallum cackled with glee. "Oh, this is going to be so much fun," he chortled. "I believe I would very much like to make this as slow and painful as possible. I only wish that Dulnear was alive to see this."

Son glanced behind the slaver king to see his friends battling his elite guards. For a brief moment, he saw Brunnlyn fighting, and the northerner's coat caught the wind as he spun to attack his opponent. It gave the boy an idea, and he turned around and ran toward his fallen friend.

"Where are you going?" Ocmallum shouted after him. "He can't help you anymore!"

Son ran past the body of Dulnear, and stopped at his friend's coat lying on the ground. "He took it off to fight the giant," he said to himself. "When he ate the berries." He then withdrew his knife and quickly cut the sleeves and hem short so that it would fit him. As he put it on, the smell of catnip was overwhelming. He then began to walk back toward the slaver king.

"Well, *there's* something you don't see every day," the old man said with a crooked grin. "Are you trying to defeat me by channeling the spirit of your dead mentor?"

Son remained silent. Instead of matching wits with the slaver, he swiped his sword upward and inward, taking off a small piece of the top of his ear, leaving it dangling like a leaf ready to fall from its branch.

Shock overtook the man's face as he reached up to attempt to reattach the piece of flesh. "What? I'll kill you!" he screeched, and plunged his sword toward the boy.

Son sidestepped and blocked each strike. The battle was reminiscent of the one he fought in Dorcadas where he first defeated the old man. With each attack and counter-attack, Ocmallum grew slower and weaker as the catnip in Dulnear's coat nullified the effects of the borb elixir. Finally, Son disarmed the man and stole his sword.

"Please! Wait!" the slaver king begged, and fell to his knees.

Son looked behind Ocmallum. He could see that his guards were defeated, and his friends were making their way back to his side.

"Don't kill me!" Ocmallum wheezed.

The boy was filled with a mixture of fury and pity. The old man besieged his home, killed his friend, and tried to kill him. However, his now frail, pathetic frame looked harmless. "Give me a good reason not to," the boy demanded.

"I can do good," the old man groveled. "I'm the wealthiest man in Aun. I can help a lot of people." He paused for a moment and added, "And you can help me by showing me who I can help."

Son considered Ocmallum's words for a moment. He longed to help others, and the brief thought of being able to give the slaver's money to the needy seemed like a valid reason for keeping him alive. "You would give it all away?" he asked.

Just then, Faymia stood by the boy's side. She was stoney-faced and unmoved by the slaver's petitions.

Standing to his feet, Ocmallum gestured toward the woman. "I could start with her," he offered. "A new house, for starters, just to say how sorry I am."

Son glanced back toward Maren, then to the slaver king. "And what about her?" he asked.

"Well, a first-class education, of course. And a new dress, and playthings."

"I know you, Son," the old man coughed. "You are good. You didn't kill me in Dorcadas when you had the chance, and you won't kill me now. You're above that sort of thing."

Son began to lower his sword. He couldn't kill a defeated foe in cold blood. Just as he began to sheath his blade, Faymia lunged forward with her dagger and plunged it into the old man's belly.

"I guess I'm just not there yet," the woman stated plainly, and watched Ocmallum drop back to his knees. He then fell to his side and his blood saturated the ground.

Son was speechless as he took a step back. He looked around and observed his companions as they watched the old man die.

## CHAPTER TWENTY-ONE

# THE TURNING OF THE TIDE

Son stood in his room doing his best to button his shirt all the way to the top. It was new, and stiff, and terribly uncomfortable. His friends were waiting for him in the garden where the memorial had been placed for his mother and for Maren's parents.

Glancing out the window, he could see the surviving Saor brethren, Henry the barkeep, Aesef, and Phel. As he watched, he could see Faymia and Maren join them.

Taking a deep breath, he willed himself to finish getting ready, slowly buttoning an ill-fitting black coat despite crushing sadness that threatened to bring him to his knees. The previous days had been spent cleaning up from the battle, rethatching the roof of the house, and taking care of the bodies of former slaves, townspeople, mercenaries, slavers, and friends.

Knowing that Dulnear was gone forever brought a stifling emptiness to the farm. It was a void that Son could feel in his chest, and he often prayed for the Great Father to fill it.

Turning from the window, he stepped outside of his room, made his way down the stairs, and out of the house to his friends. When he arrived, he could see Brunnlyn and Onclaid standing near a memorial they had made from Dulnear's sword, belt, and dagger. The rest of the group turned toward him as if waiting for him to speak, but he didn't know what to say.

Son looked at each of his friends. They all looked strangely different to him on this occasion. He cleared his throat and croaked, "Thank you for being here," then began to cry.

As he closed his eyes and wept, he could hear the sniffling and sobbing of those around him. There was a part of him that hoped that the past few days were just a dream. That he would wake up and be having the conversation with Dulnear once again to determine if they would stay and fight or flee. This time, he would choose to flee, and they would flee together, and his friend would be alive.

Clearing his throat and wiping his tears onto the sleeve of his coat, he said, "When I first met Dulnear, I didn't understand him. I told him that I didn't want to live, and for some reason, he vowed to keep me alive. I didn't realize it at the time, but he saw something in me worth committing to. It was something I surely didn't see in myself. He seemed to have a gift for seeing things in people and situations that others did not. He was a man of deep conviction. Though he often showed his shortcomings, he never wavered in the things that were important to him.

"My first morning spent with him, he had his coffee, spent time with the ancient texts, and whispered many prayers. Every morning was the same. He believed that, no matter what he faced, the Great Father was good, and that he was loved. I'm sure that, in his final moments, he did not doubt those two things.

"He taught me many lessons during our times of training. However, the most important things I learned by watching the way he lived. He was a father to me, a friend, and a mentor. My life will never be the same because of what began that day on the road to Blackcloth, and I will forever be filled with gratitude."

Finally, the grief became too much to bear and Son fell to his knees and sobbed. As he did, he felt Maren's hand on his shoulder trying to comfort him as she cried alongside him. The world spun, and he focused his thoughts to return to his feet for fear he would never be able to get up again. As he did, he could hear the deep, droning voices of the Saor as they began to sing their song of lament.

"They're singing of his bravery and valor," Maren whispered to the boy.

Son had no idea how Maren knew the words sung by the men from the north since they were singing in their native tongue. He would have asked, but was afraid that if he spoke to her, he would lose his composure once again.

"Now they're singing about a boy, a slave woman, and an orphan," she added. "I think that's us."

"I know it is," Son swallowed, gently squeezing the girl's hand.

When the song was over, Brunnlyn shared the story of how Dulnear sacrificed his hand to end the violence with his rival's family in Tuas-arum. When he was done, each of the Saor brethren told tales about their countryman. Eventually, Faymia stepped forward and shared how the man she loved purchased her from the slavers and set her free.

"He saved me in so many ways," she said. "He showed me a new way to see myself, and a new way to live." She then gestured toward Son and Maren and added, "And welcomed me into the strangest, most incredible family I could have ever asked for."

After a moment of silence, others began to share stories. Some of them, Son heard for the first time, and was surprised by them. The crowd wept, sang, laughed, and shared until the sky began to darken, and many had to make their way home.

Son said a fond farewell and gave great appreciation to Aesef and Phel as they prepared to return to Blackcloth.

"Come and visit anytime," the old farmer invited.

"I will," Son returned. "And not just when I'm in trouble."

"I'll hold you to that," Aesef smiled.

The sky became dark, and torches were lit so they could continue to visit near Dulnear's memorial. Eventually, only Son and the Saor remained.

"You are fortunate," Brunnlyn said to the boy. "Dulnear had much love for you."

"I know he did," Son replied. "I owe him so much."

"I see him in you," the man added.

Something about those words brought a small amount of comfort to the boy. "I suppose I don't yet know fully the impact he had on me. In a way, I'll still be learning from him for a long time."

"We all will," Brunnlyn exhaled.

Eventually, Son said goodnight to his northern friends,

embracing and exchanging gratitude. As he laid in his bed that night, he could hear them out in the garden singing and sharing stories until he drifted off into a deep, exhausted sleep.

In Son's dream, he opened his eyes to the rolling hills of Neahemel. Having been there once before, he recognized it immediately. The deep blue sky, the drifting clouds, and the lush, green grass carpeting the ground filled his senses.

"Stillness," the boy said out loud. It was not the dreary stillness or aching emptiness he had experienced since the Battle of Gale Hill. It was a peace that he felt in every part of his body, without lingering questions or imposing thoughts of restless tomorrows. He closed his eyes and drew in a deep breath through his nostrils, savoring the warm air and the smell of summer jasmine and lilac.

"Fancy seeing you here!" a familiar voice called out.

"Dulnear!" Son shouted. He ran to him and threw his arms around him.

The man from the north appeared younger somehow. The wrinkles of time and care were gone from his face, and even when his mouth wasn't smiling, his eyes seemed to be. His clothes were cleaner than Son had ever seen clothes look before, and he carried no possessions.

"It is good to see you, Son!" Dulnear beamed.

"And it's good to see you," Son replied. "I miss you terribly."

"Ah, I know," the man said. "It is difficult to be apart.

But our separation is not forever." He then gestured toward a nearby stone bench for them to sit on together.

The two sat and stared out over the hills, toward the vast mountains in the distance. Finally, Son started to weep.

"What is it, my boy?" Dulnear asked as he turned and placed his hand on Son's shoulder.

"It's just that... " the boy wept, "I feel like you would still be with me in Aun if I had chosen to flee instead of fight."

Dulnear gently raised Son's chin and looked into his eyes. "Please promise me something," he said.

The boy nodded.

"Promise me that you will never blame yourself for my death."

Son's shoulders began to shake and he closed his salty eyes.

"You have no more responsibility for my death than you do for my birth," Dulnear continued. "Besides, it was a glorious death, defeating a deadly foe," he added. "'Tis the goal of every man from Tuas-arum."

Opening his eyes and looking into his friend's face, Son admitted, "It's just that I thought it would be different."

"Different?"

"Yes. I thought victory against Ocmallum would be more... " the boy started, but couldn't find the words to finish.

"Victorious?"

"Yes! Victorious. I thought there would be celebrating and dancing."

"Instead, your victory carried deep sadness," Dulnear observed.

"It was all blood, and death, and ruin," Son lamented. "None of the runaway slaves even expressed thanks."

"Victory comes at a price," his friend explained. "And the greater the victory, the higher the cost."

"Was it worth it?" the boy asked as tears formed anew under his eyes.

"Slavery is over in the land of Aun," the man from the north said. "It was definitely worth it to me."

"But you died!" Son replied.

Dulnear laughed and squeezed his friend's shoulder. "Do I look dead to you? I am surrounded by the most incredible beauty I have ever seen. I am whole. There is no more conflict in me. And I am with the Great Father."

Son thought about the man's words for a moment. He remembered his encounter with the Great Father, and often longed to return to him. "Do you see him?" he asked.

"All the time," Dulnear answered. "He even gave me a new name!"

"A new name?"

"Yes!" the man said excitedly. "Dulnear is a warrior's name. There are no wars to fight here, so he calls me Rowiciel. It means healer."

Son smiled. "I like that," he exclaimed. "In many ways, you were a healer to me in Aun."

"Perhaps that is why he gave me the name," the man smiled.

Son shifted in his seat and gazed out at the landscape stretched out before him. He watched a great eagle take flight and soar into the distance, and it briefly took his breath away. Dulnear soon turned as well and the two sat side by side. Feeling spent, yet refreshed, the boy rested his head against his mentor's chest as a final tear ran down his cheek.

"I almost forgot," the man from the north added. "The Great Father told me that he is quite fond of you."

"He is?" Son murmured, then released a great sigh that he did not even know he was holding in. After some time considering his friend's words, he breathed, "Dulnear?"

"Yes."

"It was worth it."

The man from the north reached around and stroked the boy's hair gently. "I am glad to hear that. I love you, Son."

"I love you," the boy returned. "Rowiciel."

Son took a deep, cleansing breath and nestled a little further into his friend's chest. He then fell into the deepest, most peaceful sleep he had ever known.

The gray morning light spilled onto Son's face as he lay in his bed. He thought deeply about his dream, and determined to write it down so he would never forget it.

Rising from his bed, he looked out his window and saw no trace of the Saor brethren besides some smoldering coals where they had built a fire near Dulnear's memorial.

The smell of bacon arose from the kitchen, causing his mouth to water, so he threw on his clothes and ran down the stairs. Sitting at the table were Faymia and Maren. It was strange to see only the two of them since the preceding days were filled with so much commotion and company.

"There is some for you on the stove," Faymia announced.

There was sadness in her voice, and Son wished he could take it away for her. He wanted to tell her about his dream, or say anything that would make her smile, but was afraid that his words would only deepen her grief. "Thank you," was all he said as he placed some bacon and bread onto a plate and joined his friends at the table.

"Good morning," Maren greeted as she briefly looked up from her book to take a bite of food.

"Good morning," Son returned. "What are your plans today?"

"I'm showing Faymia how to ride Verrox," she answered with great enthusiasm.

"How exciting," the boy replied. "Does that mean you'll be riding Earl?"

"I suppose so," she said with much less vigor.

"I'm sure you're going to have great fun with that," Son said to Faymia with a mischievous grin.

The woman chuckled and shook her head. "I just hope the smelly beast doesn't lick my face."

Son was happy to see the woman's smile. "Bring a rag, just in case," he added.

"Brunnlyn left this morning," Maren said to Son. "So did his friends."

"I figured," the boy replied. "Did you see them before they left?"

"No, but he left a note, and some money," she answered.

"Really?" Son chirped as he raised an eyebrow.

"It said he hopes to see you again one day," the girl

explained. "And that they were taking the metal hands you made for Dulnear. That's what the money is for."

"That's odd," the boy observed. "I would have given those to them if I had known they wanted them."

The three took their time eating breakfast, then sat in front of their empty plates much longer than usual. Finally, Faymia spoke to Son. "I was sorry to hear about the passing of your father. In the midst of all the madness, I neglected to give my condolences."

Son's shoulders drooped as he listened to his friend's words. The thought of his father carried much anger and sadness for him. "No condolences needed," he said. "He is not worth them."

Faymia reached across the table and touched the boy's hand. "How you say goodbye to someone dear to you is important," she said. "Even if it's someone who wronged you."

Son considered the woman's words for a moment. He felt abandoned and betrayed by his father, but didn't want to carry the weight of it all. Pondering ways he could close that chapter of his life, he had an idea. "Will you have a memorial with me?"

"Of course," the woman replied. "When would you like to do that?"

"Tomorrow," the boy answered. "I don't have much to say about him, but maybe sleeping on it would give me some ideas."

"I'll bring flowers," Maren piped in. "Can Verrox and Earl come?"

"I guess when a man doesn't have any friends, a wild beast and a mule will do," Son chuckled. He then chose his next words carefully. "I think I would like to take my memorial speech and some of the flowers, put them in my father's old tobacco box, and bury them at his farm."

Faymia pressed her brow low and her eyes narrowed. "When would you like to do that?" she asked.

"Tomorrow, after we gather," the boy answered.

The woman took a deep breath and released it. "I'm not sure I'm ready for another journey," she lamented.

"I mean to go alone," Son stated.

The three sat staring at each other for a moment, then Maren broke in. "Would you like to take Earl?" she asked.

"Thank you for the offer, but I still have my horse," he answered. "Actually, I was thinking of walking. It will give me a chance to spend time alone with my thoughts as I think about him."

"I understand," Faymia said. "Will you be back before planting? We still have Gale Hill to think about."

"Of course," the boy promised.

———

Son sat on his bed and looked around his small room. He was still tired from a restless night of sleep, but was dressed and looking forward to his trip to the family farm. As he packed his bag for his journey, he felt strange, like he was somehow more grown up than he was just a few days ago.

His thoughts were interrupted and he was quickly brought back to the present when he saw Faymia standing at the door. He had been so deep in thought that he didn't hear her climbing the stairs. "Come in," he invited her.

"Thank you," she said as she took a couple steps in and

joined him on the edge of his bed. "I wanted to give this to you."

Son suddenly realized that Faymia was holding Dulnear's coat. It was very dear to the northerner, and had belonged to his father. He paused for a moment, moving his eyes back and forth between the coat and the woman holding it. "I... " he stammered. "I don't think I can take that."

"I hemmed it to fit you," Faymia replied. "Will you at least try it on? I cleaned it too."

The boy stood silently and tried to swallow down the growing lump he felt in his throat. As he slid his arms into the coat, he noticed that the odor of catnip was nearly gone, and was replaced by the smell of his dear friend. He sniffed the sleeve, and it almost felt as if Dulnear was standing behind him.

"It fits you well," the woman said. "And, in a way, it suits you."

Son thought about how he had rarely seen Dulnear without his coat, even on days when it seemed too warm to wear one. Feeling unworthy to keep the cherished keepsake, he began to take it off.

"No, please," Faymia pleaded. "I really want you to have it. And I believe he would want you to have it too."

Son slowly moved the fur coat back onto his shoulders and exhaled a deep, sad sigh. "Okay," he said. "I shall wear it proudly on my journey."

Faymia stood up and peered into the boy's eyes. "You did the right thing," she said.

"I know this has been hard for you," the boy returned.

"It's been hard for all of us," Faymia answered. "He was

my hero as well as my husband. I have so many stories I want to share with you when you return. But know that you did the right thing."

"Thank you," Son said with a sad smile. "I am glad that I still have you and Maren."

"And we are grateful for you," the woman returned. "Forever grateful."

Son stood by the road with Faymia and Maren, saying their goodbyes. It reminded him of the time Dulnear bid him farewell before returning to Tuas-arum. Kneeling to meet eyes with Maren, he said, "Take care of the animals, and try to have the stones moved out of the field before I return."

"I will," the girl answered. Then, reaching up to massage her ear, she added, "When will you be back?"

Son smiled and said, "I told you, before planting."

"Okay," the girl replied, looking toward the ground.

Son gently lifted Maren's chin and reassured her, "I'm only going to the farm and back. No adventures, I promise."

"Okay," she said again, and wrapped her arms around the boy's neck.

"I love you, Maren," he beamed. "You're my sister, and I'm not leaving you. I'm just going to say goodbye to my father."

Son waited for Maren to release him from her hug, which seemed like quite a long time compared to her normal standards. He then stood straight and looked at Faymia. "Thank you again for the coat."

"You're most welcome, again," she replied.

The boy stepped forward and embraced his friend. "I will be back soon. Be sure to look after Maren for me."

"Of course," the woman said. "We're going to have lots of fun, aren't we?"

To both of their surprise, Maren wasn't there. Before either of them could ask where she had gone, she was running toward them with a long stick.

"Don't forget a walking stick!" Maren called out.

Son chuckled as the girl handed him the stick. "This is a good one," he said as he tapped the end of it on the ground. "Thank you very much."

"You're welcome," Maren chirped.

"Well, I suppose I should go so I can get back," the boy exclaimed.

"I suppose," Faymia said.

Son turned away from his friends, and his home at Gale Hill Farm, and took his first steps east. As he did, he gave thanks to the Great Father for them, and for the strength to keep walking forward.

Eventually, a song began to form in his mind that moved with the rhythm of his walking stick. *Rum pum pum. Rum pum pum.*

I hope you enjoyed reading *Age of the Son*. *The Aun Series* has been deeply meaning fun for me to write and share with you. If you would like information about forthcoming projects, please visit my website, www.leebezotte.com and sign up for my e-newsletter. You can also join me on Facebook and X.

Thank you for journeying with me!

Lee Bezotte